Abou

"Some books educate, others illuminate, and still, others bring forth waves of emotion. Here, Wayne Lavender checks all these boxes and so much more. Using Dante Alighieri's 700-year-old map as a rough guide, this treatise reveals in painful yet humorous detail the state of the world's greatest experiment in democratic governance and the tragic end of the American Century. Calling this a 'must read' would be an understatement."

— Jonathan Pelto, (He/Him/His)
State Legislator and politician now college professor
Department of Philosophy and Political Science,
Quinnipiac University

"Wayne's work brilliantly summarizes the anger many Americans experienced during the Trump years while acting as a retelling of the administration's heinous politics, policies, and corruption. The book cements the Trump's administration and enablers as a clear and present danger to democracy in the United States. This is all done while utilizing an ingenious method of storytelling by overlaying those aforementioned tales of the Trump era over Dante's famous work. This is a GREAT read!"

— Paul Cappuzzo (He/Him/His)
Political Science Major & Economics Major |
History Minor
Quinnipiac Democrats | President
Quinnipiac University 2023

DANTE REDUX

TRUMP'S
TOWERING INFERNO

WAYNE LAVENDER

ILLUSTRATIONS BY
DON LANDGREN

Westphalia Press
An Imprint of the Policy Studies Organization
Washington, DC
2022

Westphalia Press
An imprint of Policy Studies Organization
1367 Connecticut Avenue NW
Washington, D.C. 20036
info@ipsonet.org

ISBN: 978-1-63723-917-9

Cover and interior design by Jeffrey Barnes
jbarnesbook.design

Daniel Gutierrez-Sandoval, Executive Director
PSO and Westphalia Press

Updated material and comments on this edition
can be found at the Westphalia Press website:
www.westphaliapress.org

For Maureen

The Perfect Model of Unconditional Love

ACKNOWLEDGEMENTS

A book, at least for me, is a communal project. My work stands on the shoulders of the great cloud of witnesses who stand by me, who have led me down the road of my personal journey. I remember teachers, professors, colleagues, authors, and lectures. They all helped shape who I am.

For this book I am indebted to these persons, who helped by giving moral support, or by reading my manuscript, or with suggestions and editorial comments. To Benjamin and Codruta, Peg and Christine, Clayton and Don, Jane and Deb, Paul and Sarah, Joe and Pete. Many thanks to Jonathan and Aaron, whose enthusiasm and suggestions pushed me through my dark moments, and to Tom and Steve, whose editorial contributions both clarified my writing and sharpened its focus.

CONTENTS

INTRODUCTION

Dante Aligheiri, hereafter referred to as Dante, published *The Divine Comedy* in 1320, one year before his death. It was his *magnus opus* and is widely thought to be one of the greatest works of world literature. It included Dante's tour of Hell where, guided by the Roman poet Virgil, he witnessed the suffering of real and fictional men and women throughout history. Reflecting on Dante got me thinking: What level of Hell and what forms of eternal punishment would the poet inflict on Donald Trump and his accomplices, were Dante alive today?

The Divine Comedy is divided it into three sections, *Inferno*, *Purgatoria* (Purgatory), and *Paradiso* (Paradise). It is a fictional account of Dante's visit through the afterlife, an allegory of the soul's journey following death and his theological understanding of what happens to us after we die. We read therein Dante's view of God, in a Christian context, through whom divine judgement is rendered, justice dispensed, and individuals sent toward punishment (*Inferno*) or reward (*Paradiso*). *Purgatoria* represents a place and opportunity for repentance and forgiveness for those on the way to *Paradiso*.

The most popular, and memorable, of these three sections is *Inferno*. Mention Dante to any well-read or learned person, and they will quickly call to mind his graphic portrayal of Hell. Although most of us have long since forgotten the details of Dante's work, many remember that he created descending levels of Hell based on the sin(s) of the condemned individual. The intensity of suffering increases as the condemned are sorted into lower levels that are closer to Satan, who is at the lowest level in the very pit of Hell. *In-*

ferno, like *Purgatoria* and *Paradiso*, consists of nine levels of punishment anchored by the 10th level, where Satan dwells.

Readers might also recall that in Dante's *Inferno,* the punishments meted out to sinners in Hell are thematically related to the worst of the sins (according to Dante himself) they committed in life. For instance, fortune-tellers and soothsayers, whom the Bible describes as false prophets and abominations for trying to see into the future, are portrayed in *Inferno* as having their heads placed on backwards, forcing them to walk blindly and unaware into their future. According to the Bible, only God should know the future.

Dante reimagines what people of his time thought conditions in Hell would be, when Hell was portrayed as a place of eternal punishments through heat and fire. Dante's *Inferno* certainly includes these conventional themes, but includes other forms of suffering and torture, as well, including a frozen lake at the ninth level of *Inferno* where the condemned are imprisoned in ice. Cold and ice are represented here as symbols of the absence of God's love and makes us consider what an actual Hell might be like—do sinners suffer in fire or ice? Which is the worst punishment: Burning, or freezing in Hell? How do Dante's imagined punishments compare with afterlife torments from other cultures, such as the punishment of Sisyphus by the Greek gods, who condemned him to pushing a large boulder uphill for eternity, only to watch it roll down to the bottom every time he reached the summit?

Dante was both a product and a representative of his culture. Born in Florence in 1265, he died in 1321. We think of this time as the Late Middle Ages, an era between the fall of Rome and rise of the Ottoman Empire and the soon-to-follow Renaissance. The Middle Ages have also been described as the *Dark Ages* because of the disorder and disarray that existed throughout Europe when life was usually short and bleak due to high rates of poverty and violence. In addition to indigence, Dante also saw capital punishment administered by various methods, including decapitation, burning at the stake, and suffocation by burial. In the last example, the condemned was tied to a post and then dropped into a hole in the ground upside down. After Last Rites (Confession, Eucharist, and Final Anointing), the order was given to fill the hole with dirt, which suffocated the convict. In addition to capital punishment, Dante witnessed other forms of state-imposed brutal torture and torment on individuals who were found guilty of breaking the law. The real-world tortures Dante witnessed provide the context and background to the suffering he imposes on the characters he places in Hell.

Dante's *Inferno* is graphic and disturbing. It is difficult for the modern reader to access and accept, but we need to remember that Dante's vision of Hell emerged from the poet's personal observation of mistreatment and torture sanctioned by civil governments as punishment to their own citizens. It is intentionally ugly, painful, and upsetting. *Inferno* is not a children's book.

Dante is guided through *Inferno* and *Purgatoria* by the great Roman poet Virgil, who is then replaced by Beatrice for the final tour of *Paradiso*, because 1) Virgil was pre-Christian and thus (in Dante's mind) unable to enter Heaven, and 2) Beatrice is Dante's muse, his inspiration for writing *The Divine Comedy* and his ideal of divine love.

For multiple reasons, it would have been easy for Dante to choose Virgil, who was a master poet, best known for his epics *The Aeneid* and the *Fourth Eclogue*. He was celebrated as the greatest Roman poet and an Italian hero. *The Aeneid* tells the legendary story of the founding of Rome by Aeneas, a survivor of Troy. Told in two parts, it resembles Homer's two great works, *The Iliad* and *The Odyssey*. The similarity between Homer's and Virgil's work was entirely intentional. Rome, as the successor to the Grecian/Alexandrian Empire, needed its own epic poem, and Virgil supplied it. He includes a section where Aeneas visits the underworld and has some of the same experiences Dante himself will later describe in *Inferno*. By selecting Virgil to be his fictional guide, Dante associates himself with the Roman poet and hoists himself to a higher status as he moves through Hell on the way to *Purgatoria* and *Paradiso*.

During his visit to Hell, Dante sees well-known men and women from history, including Judas Iscariot, Marcus Junius Brutus and Cassius Longinus, Emperor Frederick II, Cleopatra, Caiaphas, Attila, several popes, and other notable men and women. He also encounters mythological characters such as Charon, Minos, Medusa, Nessus, Jason, Cerberus, and the Minotaur, and characters from literature, like Achilles, Diomede, and Ulysses.

Readers also meet less-significant persons consigned to Hell. Most of these are people Dante knew personally who had, by various means, offended, insulted, or snubbed the poet, or who had committed acts of treason or war against Dante's beloved city of Florence. Dante, like Michelangelo, who painted personal acquaintances alongside famous historical characters, included inconsequential historical characters who are known today only because of their inclusion in *Inferno*.

The ninth and lowest level is where Dante consigns traitors. Treason, Dante believed, was the worst sin humans were capable of committing. At the ninth level, in the frozen lake mentioned above, are the betrayers of family, betrayers of country, betrayers of guests, and betrayers of benefactors. This is where Dante placed Bocca degli Abati, a Florentine nobleman who betrayed his own party and was a traitor to Florence at the Battle of Montaperti.

In the lowest reaches of the abyss we come across Dante's Satan, a three-headed monster. His torso and head stick out of the ice in which he and the others are held. Each head has a mouth which chews eternally on historical traitors: Brutus and Cassius, who turned on Julius Caesar, and Judas Iscariot, who betrayed Jesus. Brutus and Cassius have their lower portions in Lucifer's mouth, whereas Judas's legs are sticking out because his head and upper torso are being devoured. Judas suffers the more severe punishment since his sin in betraying the Christian Messiah was greater than Brutus and Cassius, who betrayed a secular ruler.

Having introduced Dante to thousands of souls condemned to an eternity of suffering in the *Inferno's* various levels, Virgil leads Dante through an opening in the rock behind Satan's body. They emerge into a large chamber, from which Dante and Virgil ascend to the earth's surface. They emerge on the opposite side of the planet from the one where they began their journey. There they see Mt. Purgatory and begin to scale the mountain that will eventually lead to Beatrice and *Paradiso*.

Inferno has inspired countless artists, musicians, and authors since its publication in 1320. There are paintings, drawings, and etchings. Common themes include cutaway views of *Inferno*, showing the nine levels of hell, scenes from *Inferno* or individual characters described within the epic poem.

In addition, there are songs, television shows, video games,

YouTube videos, and movies under the theme of *Inferno*. Spencer Tracy starred in *Dante's Inferno*, the 1935 movie loosely based on *Inferno*. The movie includes a 10-minute vision of hell that was been described by Leslie Halliwell as "One of the most unexpected, imaginative and striking pieces of cinema in Hollywood's history."

My favorite artistic depiction of *Inferno* is Rodin's sculpture *The Thinker*. Originally titled *The Poet* (French *Le Poète*), *The Thinker* is a bronze sculpture of a nude male portrayed leaning forward, his right elbow resting on his left thigh, the back of his right hand holding the weight of his chin. Rodin conceived this piece as part of his epic *The Gates of Hell* project in 1880. *The Gates of Hell* is a sculptured representation of Dante's *Inferno*. *The Thinker*, at the top of the sculpture, has come to be associated through the years with Dante himself, thus Rodin's title for this piece of work, *The Poet*, AKA Dante. There are 27 full-sized castings of *The Thinker* around the world. Each stand approximately six feet in height, including one outside of the Legion of Honor Museum in San Francisco that I saw over 40 years ago while a student in graduate school. The museum docent mentioned that Rodin had created this work of art to portray Dante looking down into his *Inferno*. Having just completed reading *The Divine Comedy*, I was drawn to the sculpture, and it has remained one of my favorite works of art ever since.

* * *

I have taken these few pages to acquaint, or reacquaint, readers with Dante's great work. I would be pleased to learn that some of you, having read this far, put this book down to learn more about Dante, *The Inferno* and *The Divine Comedy*, and the assurance of justice and accountability for malefactors they describe.

But now it's time to turn our attention to a contemporary version of the *Inferno*, in which ex-president Donald Trump and his enablers suffer the consequences for the "reign of errors and terrors" they inflicted on America. How this morally challenged leader of a family crime syndicate won the presidency and could return to the White House again on January 20, 2025—despite two impeachments—is as incomprehensible as the fact that almost no one associated with the Trump regime has been arrested, fined, imprisoned, or otherwise made to pay for their crimes.

So far. But one of these fine days . . . well, you'll just have to take the tour.

Don't worry—I'll be there with you. And who am I? Well, I consider myself to be a progressive Democrat. Born in 1957, I remember watching John Kennedy's funeral, although the images are faint and blurry. At age 11, I put my full weight (98 pounds) and political influence behind the campaign of Bobby Kennedy and was heartbroken when he was assassinated. I pivoted to Humphrey and was devastated when Richard Nixon won that tight race in 1968. Through the years, I have supported Democratic candidates for president and mourned when Republicans took the White House, gutted regulations, cut taxes for the wealthy, and waged expensive wars.

All that said, I did think that George Herbert Walker Bush ("Bush I"), the 41st president of the United States, was a decent man and an admirable leader. I also once believed that his son, George W. Bush ("Bush II" and the nation's 43rd president), was the worst president in recent decades and surely one of the worst of all time.

Then came Donald J. Trump. If you lived through these administrations, did you ever imagine that the Bush II years would come to seem, in retrospect, like a paragon of sanity and function? Me, neither. And yet, here we are.

True, Bush II was followed by eight years of Barack Obama. Obama's grace, intelligence, and oratory skills are remarkable and rare. Men and women with his charisma and leadership skills come along once in a lifetime. Unfortunately, the U.S. electorate only gave him two years to partner with Democratic leadership in Congress. Three-fourths of the time he was in office, Obama had to struggle against hostile and obstructionist legislators, thus limiting the good he might otherwise have been able to achieve during his presidency. Many of those same legislators have been, and still are, Trump boosters.

Go figure. Obama is out of office. They aren't. There are scores that cry out for settlement that don't seem to be getting traction at the ballot box.

But maybe someday, what goes around will come around. What might that look like, if so? Read on and see for yourself.

Now, as a modern Christian, I don't *really* think that Hell is an actual place, or that God literally metes out everlasting torment, even for ferociously screwing up what we have and have not done, in the great scheme of our pretty short lives. The God in whom I trust is a God of grace and peace, mercy, and love.

As a parent myself, I love my children deeply, even when they behave in ways of which I disapprove. Even if I had the power to do it, I would never even consider sending one of my children, at their absolute worst, to suffer everlasting punishment in Hell. If I am capable of compassion and grace rather than anger and vengeance, surely God is even more so.

Does that mean I think everyone goes to Heaven? Truthfully, I'm not so sure about Heaven, either. As a person of deep and abiding faith, I have come to realize that this faith comes and goes daily. I've found living right here on earth in the 20th and 21st centuries challenging and rewarding in equal measure. I've also discovered comfort and meaning in living my life with a diverse group of faith-based people who have patiently shaped me and supported me over the decades. I do the best I can and will let the afterlife sort itself out.

The God I believe in, and hope exists, is the God described throughout the Bible who from the opening paragraphs of Genesis to the final chapter of Revelations has a love of all people, with a focused and preferential treatment for the poor. Thus, "The Church's love for the poor . . . is a part of her constant tradition. This love is inspired by the Gospel of the Beatitudes, of the poverty of Jesus, and of His concern for the poor" (Conscientia and Annus 2019).

As a Christian, I am commanded, mandated, charged, instructed, pick your verb, to love and care for the least, the last and the lost—to feed the hungry, provide water to the thirsty, clothing to the naked, and to visit the sick and those in prison. This is not an option for people of faith, be they Christian, Muslim or Jew, or any other world religion. Caring for orphans, widows and foreigners is in our DNA. It is not only expected for persons of faith, it also itself brings its own rewards and benefits. If my eternal retirement benefits put me at the great banquet where we are reunited with saints and family members, so much the better.

A mean spirited, angry, judgmental and hate filled Christian is not a Christian in this book. It is that simple, really.

So, I wrote this book as an allegory, a parody, a travelogue of an afterlife I do not pretend for a second is real, but which might nevertheless provide readers some comfort. I wish I could claim to be breaking new ground in doing this, but not only do I borrow Dante in this book, I also want to add a scroll to the apocalyptic tradition of Ezekiel, Daniel, and Revelation. The writers of those books also lived in dangerous times under despotic leaders (Pharaoh, Nebuchadnezzar, and Nero, respectively) who made others suffer through their misdeeds but never seemed to suffer themselves. Apocalyptic writers in each of these turbulent times urged their faithful readers to hang on and assured their readers that the wicked *will* get what's coming to them, and when they do, well, maybe it will look like this or that or the other thing.

That's what I'm up to, here. Reader, justice won't slumber forever. Trump and his allies have wreaked havoc on our nation and world and continue to endanger it. One of these days, though, Justice will be served. Possibly with Hellfire. Or with some other, more creative recompense. We don't really know when, and we don't really know how, but we know it *will* happen.

One more thing: I don't use the word *evil* lightly. The dictionary definition of evil includes "morally reprehensible, sinful, wicked" (e.g., "an evil impulse") and "arising from actual or imputed bad character or conduct" (e.g., "a person of evil reputation.") In the book *People of the Lie,* psychologist Scott Peck describes "evil" as the willful embrace of untruth. (Peck 1983) I don't want to see "evil" cheapened by association with mere drunkenness, laziness, stupidity, or impulsive violence. I want to reserve "evil" for extreme cases—like the Trump presidency.

The basis for Trump's serial lying and actions stems in part from his narcissism. "Since [narcissists] deep down, feel themselves to be faultless, it is inevitable that when they are in conflict with the world they will invariably perceive the conflict as the world's fault. Since they must deny their own badness, they must perceive others as bad. They project their own evil onto the world. They never think of themselves as evil, on the other hand, they consequently see much evil in others." (Peck 1983)

What word can better capture the actions and legacy of the Trump presidency? From appointing incompetent toadies to important offices, to petty vengefulness in policy choices, to setting a standard of anger, racism, and hatred imitated across the United States and around the world, we have not seen the like of the administration's callousness and self-serving.

The former president is himself a walking dictionary definition of the classical cardinal sins, a non-Biblical grouping of vices defined within the Christian tradition, including lust (Stormy Daniels,), gluttony (he is morbidly obsess from a steady diet of junk food), greed (overcharges for government events held on Trump properties), sloth (no need to read briefings, in fact, no need to read at all and "morning" = 12 noon), wrath (James Comey and Mike Pence can tell you about crossing the boss), envy ("if only I could be like Putin …"), and pride (Trump is the definition of "braggart"). Others have diagnosed him as a narcissist, racist, misogynist, xenophobe, and pathological liar. The answer to the question, "How can you tell when Donald Trump is lying?" is simple: "Whenever his mouth is open and he's talking."

Trump and his administration took lying to a whole new level. According to the fact checker from *The Washington Post*, Trump told a total of 30,573 lies during his four years in office, an average of 21 per day (Kessler, Rizzo, and Kelly, 2021). Trump's lying reminds me of the quote attributed to Aleksandr Isayevich Solzhenitsyn, who wrote: "We know they are lying, they know they are lying, they know we know they are lying, we know they know we know they are lying, but they are still lying."

Trump began his administration with the Small Lie about the size of the crowd gathered at his inauguration (it was much smaller than he and his press secretary and senior advisors claimed). We know these were lies because there is empirical evidence showing the truth. He ended his time in office with the Big Lie about the 2020 election. In between were the 30,000+ lies. Trump's press secretaries, Sean Spicer, Sarah Huckabee, and Kailey McNerney brought lying to a whole new level during their official briefings. Right in front of our eyes, the White House was transformed into the Lie House.

This penchant for lying has spread through the Republican Party. Note the ease with which Kevin McCarthy lied about comments he made to colleagues on January 10, 2021, when he said he would urge Trump to resign over the January 6 attack at the Capitol Building in Washington, D.C. (Martin and Burns 2022) Other notable liars within the Republican camp include Senators such as Mitch McConnell, Lindsay Graham, Ted Cruz, and Josh Hawley, and governors like Ron DeSantis and Greg Abbott. We will run into these characters again in *Trump's Towering Inferno*.

I don't know if we are living in a world where truth and speaking the truth still matter. However, we are living during a time where one political party has willfully chosen to disregard facts and the truth. Their claims that night is day, black is white, peace is war and up is down go unchallenged by their base. Orwell and countless others warned us against this kind of propaganda.

Our founding fathers were greatly concerned about the emergence of a demagogue who could win popular support, so they created a series of checks and balances to keep such a person from exercising such power. Madison's "Ambition must be made to counteract ambition" (Hamilton, Madison, and Jay 1982:316) comes to mind. But they never anticipated a Senate Majority leader like Mitch McConnel and his cohort, whose own ambition for power and wealth coincided with the executive office and thus allowed the president to consistently lie and deceive to the nation.

Trump's lies led not only to the insurgency and attack on the U.S. Capitol on January 6, but the spread of "The Great Lie" by his enablers and base. In response, Republican-led states have passed laws to suppress votes, gerrymander districts to favor Republicans and provide legislative bodies the ability to overturn election results. Trump and his allies present the greatest threat to democracy and the great American Experiment that we have faced since the ratification of the Constitution in 1788. Ben Franklin's reply to the woman who asked him what form of government had been created received this answer from the respected Founding Father: "A republic if you will keep it." The forces to end the republic are alive and among us today and are leading the Republican Party of Donald Trump.

In addition, racism had a great resurgence during the Trump Administration. Systemic racism is as American as baseball and apple pie. The settling of our nation took coincided with the intentional, genocidal campaign against the First Nation People who had settled here centuries before Europeans arrived, and that settlement by Europeans was built on slavery. Racism was then ingrained into our Constitution. Ten of our first 12 presidents owned slaves, further normalizing that insidious institution in our collective memory and identity. Although it is clear that not all Republicans are racists, it is also clear that the Republican Party has done more to sustain the status-quo of racism within our nation than the Democratic Party, who puts forth programs and policies that favor dismantling racism.

Trump sprinkled racist comments throughout his campaign and administration. His administration employed well-known racists and saw a dramatic rise in racist attacks against Jews, Muslims, and persons of color. The number of hate crimes in this nation continues to climb.

So, "evil?" Yes. "Liar?" Definitely. "Racist?" Of course. But perhaps the single most appropriate word I would use to describe Donald Trump is this: *Traitor*. He has been a traitor to his oath of office, to the Constitution, and the people of the United States. To argue otherwise is to take the losing side. More details to follow will include:

1. His disdain and disregard of the emoluments clause of the U.S. Constitution and focus on his own profit and personal needs in his perverse abuse of power and corruption.

2. His siding with Russian president Vladimir Putin over U.S. intelligence agencies.

3. His ongoing disinformation campaign denying the dangers of the COVID-19 virus, leading to the death of over one million U.S. citizens.

4. His vehement and racially motivated opposition to immigration and path to citizenship for millions of worthy and deserving people. "The bosom of

America is open to receive not only the opulent and respectable Stranger, but the oppressed and persecuted of all Nations and Religions," said George Washington to Joshua Holmes in 1783. (Meacham 2018:82) Having married two immigrants himself, Trump's angry attacks on immigrants of color and repeated promises to "build the wall" stand in opposition to the concept President Kennedy used, and what is a historical reality, to describe the United States as a "nation of immigrants." It was President Reagan who, in his final speech as president, said this: "If we ever closed the door to new Americans, our leadership in the world would soon be lost." Trump's antiimmigrant words and policies have hurt the United States of America and made us a weaker nation.

5. His role in the insurrection against the United States on January 6, 2021.

For these and other reasons, I have created a modern version of Dante's *Inferno* and have named it *Trump's Towering Inferno*. Like Dante's *Inferno*, I have created a nine-level depiction of Hell devoted to Donald Trump and his cohort of supporters and enablers. Unlike Dante, this *Inferno* does not go down into the earth toward Lucifer and the lowest level of Hell, but up, inside Trump Tower, where the worst offenders are placed higher in the building, with Donald Trump himself found above the ninth level.

I have chosen, as my guide through my *Trump's Towering Inferno*, Benedict Arnold, heretofore remembered in history as the greatest American traitor. Arnold, a native of Connecticut, fought bravely and well for the emerging nation before souring on the revolutionary spirit and turning against George Washington, his native nation, and its cause of freedom. As the commander of West Point, he provided detailed information to the British forces of Washington's movements and made plans for West Point to be surrendered to the British. After his plans were discovered, he escaped to New York City. The British, recognizing his military brilliance, promoted him to brigadier general. He led military raids in Virginia and then, later, in Connecticut, near where he was born and raised. In December 1781, he and his family boarded a ship bound for England, where he died in 1801.

In the future, a year from now, a decade, 20, 50, and 100 years down the road, and more, Donald J. Trump's name will be remembered and his legacy of nepotism, incompetence, criminal negligence, racism, misogyny, xenophobia, narcistic personality disorder, and traitorous behavior firmly cemented. In fact, it is possible we will soon and thereafter be referring to, first, individuals whose self-love and devotion to themselves make it impossible to see beyond their own interests and desires as persons who have *Trump Personality Disorder,* replacing *narcistic behavior disorder,* and second, describe any individual who engages in traitorous behavior as a contemporary Donald J. Trump.

But time will blur the memory and record of those who enabled this soulless, corrupt, serial adulterer, and pathological liar to win the most powerful position on the planet and spew venom on Twitter and in speeches, interviews, public policy, executive orders, and laws. Better to document their complicity with this child-monster now than have them slip away to the footnotes of history.

In a way, Donald J. Trump is merely the tip of the iceberg of what is wrong in the United States. Time and space will not allow for a complete listing of those whose support made these four years of Hell on earth possible as the list is long and still growing. The personality cult that has developed around this man is difficult to understand for those of us immune to its influence. Those under his sway include approximately 30 percent of the American public. This is the core of the Republican Party. Most Republican leaders alternate between a personal hatred of this man to public praise as profiles in cowardice. We know this because we have the tapes—audio and video. But somehow, they always slink back to this demagogue who clearly suffers from psychological and emotional health issues.

Plenty of academic and well-researched books have already been written bringing light to Trump, his family, administration, and business. These books have been written from those within and outside the Trump circle. However, his base continues to be unmoved.

Consider the book *A Sacred Oath*, by Mark Esper (Esper 2022). Esper served as the U.S. secretary of defense *appointed* by Donald Trump. A bona fide Republican, he is a West Point graduate who saw combat duty during the Gulf War. Following his military service, he served as the chief of staff for the Heritage Foundation, one of the most influential conservative think tanks in the nation. He ricocheted around the military-industrial-political complex, working as a congressional staffer and senior executive and lobbyist for defense contractors. Prior to his elevation to secretary of defense, Esper served as secretary of the Army.

In his book, published in May 2022, Esper claims that Trump asked him on several occasions to "shoot missiles into Mexico to destroy the drug labs" and "no one would know it was us." Further, he wrote, regarding the George

Floyd protestors, "Can't you just shoot them?" Finally, Esper concluded that Trump is "an unprincipled person who, given his self-interest, should not be in the position of public service."

Where is the hue and cry from every American regarding these revelations? Note that Esper is no MSNBC or *Huffington Post* reporter, but an insider who saw crazy up close and personal. This book alone should disqualify Trump from ever getting votes again at any level of public service. And yet …

I am not, sadly, a poet, and, unfortunately, I am aware of this fact. But I have chosen, in the spirit of Dante, to begin each chapter with a short poem, a rewriting of a nursery rhyme to set the stage and remind us of Dante's greatness.

Some will find this book graphic and difficult to read. Others will find it therapeutic and liberating. Certain readers will find it difficult to read *and* therapeutic. Like Dante's *Inferno*, this is *not* a children's book. It is often dark and depressing. *Trump's Towering Inferno* is not for the faint of heart or squeamish. It will take readers through many of the extraordinarily difficult and dark days and events of the Trump years, which can trigger PTSD-type responses. Some will read this book straight through and finish it in an afternoon or evening, while others will need to put it down and walk away from it, maybe returning after a short or long break, maybe not. Reader beware: again, this is *not* a children's book.

This IS a book for those who, like me, believe that there will be justice, in this life or the next. And it presents an alternative reality, a glimpse into how persons of faith can practice their religion using the gifts of grace and peace, mercy, and love. Finally, it is a book I believe lies at the nexus of fiction, academia, and prophecy. It was George Santayana who said, "Those who cannot remember the past are condemned to repeat it."

I never imagined writing this book, but the events of the past few years have compelled me to do so. This is my first work of fiction, a labor of conscience and written out of my sense of right and wrong. Researching this book brought me face to face with the words and actions of "The Donald" and his associates. Donald J. Trump and his movement were, and remain today, a clear and present threat to democracy and the great American Experiment. I wrote this book not because I wanted to but because it welled up from within and because it burst out of me after living through this Trumpian reign of terror. I also wrote this book, if for no other reason, as an act of personal trauma healing. And, finally, I wrote this book as a word of warning that as the 2022 midterm and 2024 presidential elections draw nigh, we must never forget the un-American and undemocratic ideals and principles that Donald Trump and his supporters stood for—and still stand for.

I dearly understand that this book will not, unlike Dante's, be read 100 or 500 years from now, or, like Virgil's works, be read 2,000 years into the future. This is simply my humble attempt to bring together, under the unifying theme of Dante's *Inferno*, the bad men and women who enabled Donald Trump to become the president of the United States and aided his disgraceful and traitorous reign. We study the past to inform our present and shape the future. Let us therefore remember this dark time in U.S. history in order to create a future free from the racism, xenophobia, corruption, misogyny, and hatred of this *enfant terrible*.

CHAPTER 1

THE STEPPING STONES

Frumpty Trumpty sat on a wall
With all of his cronies at his beck and call.
"I won the election, this doesn't make sense
Let's storm the capitol and hang Mike Pence."

His text, like the others, was succinct: "Tomorrow, high noon, bottom of the moving staircase."

After a week of receiving texts from a man who died more than 200 years ago, I was no longer surprised, but still suspicious and uncertain about my next move. "To meet, or not to meet?" That was the question that kept me awake. Finally, though, I'd made my decision. Someone identifying themselves as none other than General Benedict Arnold worked very hard to set up a meeting with me. Why not go along and see what he has in mind and why he wants me to meet with him?

I arrived almost an hour early on Friday, April 2, 2021. Trump Tower, located at 725 Fifth Avenue in New York City, is easy to find and close to many other landmarks in New York. It is just a few blocks north of St. Patrick's Cathedral and only a few miles from where Alexander Hamilton was mortally wounded (at the dueling grounds on the western shore of the Hudson River) by Aaron Burr, and even closer to where Hamilton died the next day. Trump Tower is four miles north of the Federal Building, where George Washington took the oath of office to become the first president of the United States, and about a mile north of the Empire State Building, once the tallest building in New York City. It is also five miles north of the 9/11 Memorial and site of the original World Trade Center. Trump Tower is about six miles, as the crow flies, from where the Statue of Liberty stands on Liberty Island, and approximately four miles south of Grant's Tomb, where General and Mrs. Grant lie. Many other landmarks and historical sites are nearby.

Dueling protesters waged a fierce, verbal battle outside the enormous bronze-framed glass doors that serve as the main entrance to Trump Tower. On one side of the barricades were the Trump supporters, waving Trump and American flags and signs blaring messages like, "Biden Stole the Election!" "COVID Is A Hoax—End Mask Mandates!" and "Hang Mike Pence!" Still seething from their beloved leader's loss at the polling booths, caused by their imagined voter fraud and a corrupt, anti-Trump, Deep State bureaucracy, they were loaded for bear and looking for a fight.

Separated from the faithful by a throng of New York City police officers was an equally large crowd of anti-Trumpers. Equally as bellicose as the MAGA crowd, this group waved their own placards that supported causes such as Black Lives Matter, calls for investigation into the January 6 insurrection at the U.S. Capitol building, environmental issues, and pleas for imprisonment for members of Trump's administration, his family, and the former president himself ("Lock Him [Trump] Up!")

I circled the building to get the lay of the land before I entered the Tower. Away from the demonstrators, all was typically Manhattan. I saw hot dog and pretzel stands next to taco trucks and ice cream vendors. Fifth Avenue was lined with upscale retail stores selling jewelry, clothing, computers, and more, most with guards posted inside the doorways to protect their businesses. Sidewalks were crowded with New Yorkers of all kinds, from men and women dressed in business clothing to others more casually attired. Joggers weaved and dodged through the crowds. Tourists from the U.S., Europe, and Asia took photos and videos of landmarks and the people near them.

Returning to the front of the building, I read the directory of the Trump Atrium: Trump Bar, Trump Grill, Trump Café, Trump's Ice Cream Parlor, the Trump Store, and Trump Events at the Atrium. I made a wry face. Trump is everything and everything is Trump here in the Tower. Well, of course.

No directory pointed to Trump chaos, Trump turmoil, or Trump conflicts, but I understood I was at the wellhead for so much that had roiled the United States since Donald J. Trump emerged as his party's leader more than four years earlier. Heedless of the angry rhetoric hurled back and forth on the street in front of Trump Tower, I stepped through the police lines and entered the building.

I knew immediately I was a pilgrim in an unholy land. Should I take off my shoes in deference? Nah, that didn't seem right. Put my shoes to work escaping from Trump Tower? That seemed a lot more reasonable. But I was meeting someone. I pushed my misgivings aside and pushed on.

Before me was the grand escalator Melania and Donald Trump descended on June 16, 2015, when The Donald announced that he would be running for president in 2016. The escalator was an anchor feature of the whole atrium, a large room with lots of windows, mirrors, and shiny metallic walls. An electronic display that looked a lot like the news signage in Times Square circled the atrium. The message, "All hope must be checked at the door if you cross this threshold," chased itself around the perimeter of the room.

I focused my attention on the foot of the escalator where, as promised, an average-sized man in a faded military uniform stood waiting. His clothing was frayed at the edges and scorched in several spots. He stood stiffly straight, a soldier out of his comfort zone in a strange civilian world.

Suddenly, I noticed that the floor between me and the escalator was packed with heads. They rose from the floor, chock-a-block as though the hidden necks did not attach to shoulders and bodies below floor level. There were heads fully covered with hair, balding heads, and bald heads. Women's heads and men's heads were packed in straight rows and lines, exposed from the chins up. It was like a carpet of human heads, all with open eyes staring blankly at the back of the head in front of them. Hundreds of heads were literally cheek to cheek, ear to ear, and nose to nape.

Not every head was disembodied. Dozens of full-bodied, fully dressed U.S. Capitol police officers paced systematically back and forth across the room, shifting their weight from head-to-head as they marched. Faces at floor level screwed up in discomfort as the officers passed. Sharp cries of pain and anger were not uncommon. When officers reached one wall, they pivoted and went back the other direction, walking a pattern that ensured everyone in the room was stepped on regularly. Cries and muffled sobs rose from every quarter. From time to time, an officer delivered a swift kick to the front or back of one of the heads. Every face showed signs of punishment, from black and swollen eyes, to broken noses, missing teeth, and dripping blood.

The man at the bottom of the escalator had noticed me and motioned for me to join him at the escalator. I hesitated. Could I really get there by walking on human heads as if they were steppingstones?

General Arnold grimaced at my hesitation, reading it for the weakness of resolve it was. Marching deliberately, with a military cadence, my contact headed toward me across the slightly uneven "carpet" on the floor.

He stood before me, saluted, saying the words, "General Benedict Arnold, at your service." He added, "As you have seen, it's not as hard to walk on the heads as you might think."

I shook his hand in return. "Wayne," I said. "Wayne Lavender." I looked the general and his attire up and down. Arnold wore a ruffled white linen shirt under a yellow woolen vest. Over his shoulders was draped a blue jacket with yellow trim and brass buttons that sported the insignia and tassels of a general. Arnold's pants were yellow wool, with buttons to close the fly.

He wore black boots and a tri-cornered black hat. He looked a lot like artists' renderings of George Washington, but, well, livelier, with dark hair and striking brown eyes.

"Please, General Arnold," I said, glancing nervously down at the heads on the floor, "tell me what the Hell is going on here. And who, really, are you?"

"Funny you should use that word, 'Hell,'" he replied. "Hell. Hmmm. Well, as I said in my texts this past week, I am here to be your guide on a tour of *Trump's Towering Inferno.*" He poked me in the ribs with an elbow. "Get it? Like Dante's *Inferno,* except it's a tower instead of a mineshaft. I'm going to show you some places in this Tower the general public doesn't get to see: These are the floors and corridors to which the former president and his colleagues are remanded for all eternity to suffer for their crimes." This was exactly what the General had promised in the texts I had received all week, but . . . Wow. And how? "Um, General, this is all very unlikely and unbelievable. How do I know this isn't some weird dream, and it only seems like we've been texting? But this is really last Saturday and I'm still asleep."

"Does it really matter?" he responded with a tired smile. "Dreams or visions? Faith and doubt? Everything fits together, but not the way anyone thinks. What we know and what we see are just bits of a bigger reality than any but the divine mind can imagine. So, just . . . observe. Walk with me for a bit and see what I'd like to show you. There's a lot to see in *Trump's Towering Inferno,* maybe more than you have stomach for. If at any time you want to stop, just say so, and I will return you back to the street and you can resume to your regularly scheduled life."

"Um, okay," I stammered.

The General cleared his throat, as if to begin narrating from his memorized script. "I am, as stated, Benedict Arnold. Brigadier General, His Majesty King George's Army, formerly Major General, American Continental Army. You are standing in *Trump's Towering Inferno,* where I will be your guide. Should you wish to see them, I will show you the nine levels of this Hellhole and the men and women herein imprisoned for their unfailing loyalty to the worst traitor in U.S. history since, well, since 1780."

"But wait . . . Trump and his minions are still alive. Well, most of them. Anyway, how do you plan to show me the eternal torments of people who are still out there creating temporal torments for the living?"

The General shrugged. "Avatars, of course." He lifted his eyebrows, taking an almost merry expression as he caught my eyes. "What, you think Pixar has all that technology? Have no fear. But anyway, it's a good thing we have time to prepare

Benedict Arnold

the *Towering Inferno* for full occupancy in the future. We can dial in the discomfort level of every torment so it's a perfect match to the nervous system of each Trumpian decedent when they arrive. Or, I guess I should say, 'mismatch.'"

"So, what are you? The manager? The janitor at Trump Power? Are you some kind of ghost from Christmas past, here to warn me against switching to the other side of the aisle? Because I gotta tell you, you don't need to trouble yourself. I can barely stand to be in the same country with Josh Hawley or Marjorie Taylor Greene, much less the same party."

"Ah, Dickens," Arnold sighed. "No, Dickens was a novelist who wrote fiction. Great fiction, 'word,' as the kids say, but fiction never-the-less. I know of his ghosts of Christmas Past, Present, and Future, but no, I'm not a ghost. I am your guide to *Trump's Towering Inferno*. This is my penance for my own treason: To reveal what awaits those who betray America under the MAGA banner."

I gestured to the space around us. "Are these the shadows of the things that will be, or are they shadows of things that only may be?" I was a bit proud of my ability to call up a direct quote from English literature I hadn't looked at since college.

The General snorted. "Again, with your Dickens," he said. "Well, okay. If we were to come at this like Dickens, we'd say that what you are going to see today is a glimpse of what can, and will, happen in the future, circa 2080, when the Trump cast of characters have all passed from the world scene and have been judged by Americans, history, and the Almighty. That's when *Trump's Towering Inferno* will reach full occupancy. Trump's properties should be so full.

"Is this place *necessary*? Does it *have* to be? No. But c'mon, you've met many of the people you will see here, and you know they're set in their ways and not going to change. God, you know, has a great capacity and reservoir of love and grace, but will pass judgment when necessary. And here, God has taken a stand. Ted Cruz isn't going see the light. Sorry."

"Do not be deceived; God is not mocked, for you reap whatever you sow," I said, whipping off another direct quote, this time from the Bible rather than Dickens.

"Exactly. Trump sowed hatred and division. He used and stroked racism, sexism, and xenophobia. He worshipped himself and had an endless appetite for power, fame, and fortune. He was the walking opposite of Jesus's words, 'Blessed are the meek,' and Emma Lazarus's poetic ideal of what America stands for:

> Keep, ancient lands, your storied pomp!' cries she
> With silent lips. 'Give me your tired, your poor,
> Your huddled masses yearning to breathe free,
> The wretched refuse of your teeming shore.
> Send these, the homeless, tempest-tost to me,
> I lift my lamp beside the golden door!

"That's what should be posted along the southern border, instead of that stupid wall. But anyway, here is the reality. There are many self-focused, power-, fame- and fortune-seeking individuals in the United States and around the world. But most of them have no podium, elected or otherwise, and pose no threat to the United States or the world. Donald Trump, however, did have a prestigious public office, a wide base of support, and was and is a threat to the U.S. and the world. Donald Trump galvanized the anger and bitterness of just under half the nation's voters in 2016 and used his power and resources to shove a political agenda straight out of the 1950s down the throats of an electorate he despises—and those are just the ones who voted for him. You should hear what he has to say about Democrats and blue-staters!

"Of course, Trump would not, and could not, have done the harm he did by himself. He was elevated and propped up by his base, of course, but also by legitimately elected leaders and persons he appointed to positions of power within his businesses and administration, most of whom knew better than to take directions from Trump. Yet they eagerly passed Trump's lies to their own supporters and then followed him down the garden path with their own followers in tow. We know, I know, personally, that politicians lie and distort reality. But the ability of Trump and his MAGA supporters to lie, to shape-shift on policies, to defend the undefendable, take hypothetical positions and project their flaws and weaknesses to their political and social enemies is unparalleled in the history of the United States. The men and women who supported Donald Trump themselves have been judged by the maker with swift and harsh sentences."

Arnold was on a roll. I did not want to interrupt him.

"Think of Lindsay Graham," he sniffed, his words dripping with malice. "Here are a few quotes from Graham in 2015 as Donald Trump was running in the Republican primaries: 'He's a race-baiting, xenophobic religious bigot,' and 'Do you know how to make America great again? Tell Donald Trump to go to Hell.' Ha! If Donald Trump is going to Hell, it will be with a large group that helped him get to the top, including Lindsay Graham, who knew Donald Trump, was no friend of Donald Trump, knew what Donald Trump was all about (we have the videotapes!) but, for political purposes, betrayed what he knew was true and sold his soul in the process, a traitor to his own nation, political party and people."

"But wait . . . weren't *you* a traitor?"

Arnold grimaced. "Yes, of course," he said. "After years of fighting for independence, putting my own money into the revolution, and being wounded multiple times, I lost heart. I betrayed my nation and my people, and my friend, George Washington himself, who placed great faith and trust in me.

"I deeply regret what I did and died with the knowledge that what I did was wrong. My last words revealed to the world my true feeling and remorse, when I said 'Let me die in the old uniform in which I fought my battles for freedom. May God forgive me for putting on another.' I sought forgiveness." With a flip of his hands at chest level, he indicated his present attire. "This is that uniform. My body is comforted. My soul is still tormented."

"So you are in Hell, too."

"Haven't you read your Dante? Hell is for the blind, and not those who see. I earned a ticket to Hell, that's for sure, but I'm making amends. I am working my way through my past toward a better eternity nowhere near *Trump's Towering Inferno*. Confession, repentance, contrition, humility—these are available and possible for everyone. There is a way to stay out of Hell, you see, but only for those willing to turn around and find another path."

"So, the people we see here?" I asked.

"All had the freedom of choice," he replied. "This is a picture of what will happen to those who continue on their current paths. You see, ambition is not bad, but blind ambition is. Repeating the lies of The Donald and following him when you understood him and the damage he was creating was wrong. Full stop. This tour will allow you to see and then share with the world what the future will be like for those who know better but continue down this path toward eternal sorrow. Let those with ears hear."

I rubbed my palms and nodded. "Okay! So, what's next?"

"A tour of the building," he replied. "Nine stories of Hell on Earth, starting here in the lobby. The lobby is where the men and women who supported Donald Trump through his business and TV careers have been placed for eternal punishment. They knew who Trump was and still boosted him up. Here you will see these individuals being stepped on, because they stepped on whomever was in their way to climb the ladder of success. Look over to your right. That's Allen Weisselberg, who cooked the books for the Trump Organization for decades."

"Behind Weisselberg, you can see Jeffrey Epstein and Ghislaine Maxwell. Think of the conspiracy theories that gained traction during the Trump administration. First, and foremost, among these conspiracies is Q-Anon. And what was Q-Anon's most pressing and persistent claim: That within the Democratic organization is a powerful cabal of Satanic, cannibalistic pedophiles running a global child sex-trafficking ring," Arnold stated. "The irony here is rich, wouldn't you say? Donald Trump hung out with Jeffrey Epstein, one of the most famous and most prolific pedophiles in history. That's thanks to Ghislaine, Epstein's groomer and procurer. There they are. Stepped on. Kicked in the face. They are disgusting characters, like the others you will see here and within this building.

"Many of the heads you see in this lobby were Trump supporters who spread the lies he spoke and sold regarding his hotels, casinos, golf courses, beauty pageants, university, airline, wine, clothing, steak, and more. Trump is, among other things, a con man of epic proportions. Most within his orbit knew this. But they went along anyway and helped prop him up for their own personal gain and selfish ambition, scheming that some of his extraordinary luck and wealth might be their own. Well, it is, now, but not at all what they expected. They are here to be seen, forever underfoot, suffering, and stepped on, just like those they stepped on. Call it karma or what comes around goes around or reaping what you have sown: this is Trump's first level of Hell."

"Who is that man right in front of us?" I asked, "He looks somewhat familiar."

"Why don't you ask him yourself?"

I hesitated. Speaking to a living dead person imprisoned in Hell was *way* out of my comfort zone. Then again, maybe the trampled head was an avatar and not a person at all. I glanced up at the general, who nodded encouragement.

I took a step forward. This head, swollen from the steps and kicks of the guards, occupied a place that was either fortunate or unfortunate, depending on who did the assessing. As front and center on the first row in the lobby, it seemed destined to be noticed, stepped on, or kicked by every person coming into the building.

I crouched, though still could not catch the sufferer's eyes. "Sir," I whispered, "who are you? Your face seems familiar, though I'm sorry to say I can't recall your name. Maybe I saw you before in the news or in person?"

The sufferer's expression darkened with anger. "You should know me," he barked. "I am Fred Trump, father of Donald Trump! I built a real estate empire in Queens and taught my son everything he needed to know on how to be successful. I was a great businessman—once called the Henry Ford of the home-building industry. I passed my genes and DNA onto Donny and gave him my empire, smarts, and drive to get to the top."

"Ah, yes," I responded. "I recognize you now. But I also remember reading some, um, less savory parts of your resume. Weren't you arrested at a KKK rally in 1927?"

"Fake news. Fake. Fake. Fake. I was not even in New York City at the time of that rally."

Arnold stamped his foot and snorted.

"And weren't you in trouble with the Federal government for profiteering, taking governmental funding and using it to construct your housing but then overcharging for your units? And I also read . . ."

"No, no, and no," he interrupted, "I was only . . ."

The general stepped forward and placed his boot squarely on Fred's head. He proceeded to grind his heel into his skull for a few seconds. "Let my friend finish his question."

I nodded gratefully. "And I also read that you had violated some civil rights laws by not selling your housing units to people of color."

"Fake. Not true. You can't believe what you read or listen to," he snapped. Fred glanced up at General Arnold. "That hurts, damn it."

"As I intended," Arnold replied coolly.

"And," I asked, "Didn't you give a huge sum of money, in the range of $400 million in today's currency, much of it illegally, to your son Donald, to get him started in business? I have also read that you constantly hammered home a message of success, and how he should never accept anything but victory. Win. Win. Win, you taught him, no matter what the cost or price. The ends justify the means."

"I legally helped my son get his business started. Everything I gave him was appropriately reported, assessed, and taxed. And I encouraged all of my children to be successful, to strive for the best. Is there anything wrong with that?"

His angry self-righteousness disgusted me, yet I felt sorry for Fred. He could not have predicted the monster he nurtured. His like had never existed previously. All the same ... I wanted to get away from him and move on. I reflexively took a few backward steps to the outside door where I had just entered.

"What will happen to Fred?" I asked Arnold. "I mean, that's really him, not an avatar. Will he suffer eternal punishment here? He just seems like an angry, misguided, and unfriendly person. Does a bad disposition make him so evil that he will be stepped on by everyone coming and going from this building in perpetuity?"

As if on cue, one of the Capital Hill police officers came by and enthusiastically jumped atop Fred's head with both feet, then laughed as he moved on.

"Fred was no worse than any other person born on this planet, but he chose to cast his lot with evil. Remember your Solzhenitsyn," he said. "'The line dividing good and evil cuts through the heart of every human being' (Solzhenitsyn 1973, 168). Fred chose the evil. He cheated on his taxes and taught his children to do the same. He cheated on his wife. He cheated his workers and those he did business with. He bribed local politicians to make larger profits. He made millions—hundreds of millions, really—by taking federal subsidies and then overcharging his tenants. Seriously, how much money does a person really need? In addition, Fred was a bona fide racist, an anti-Semite, anti-Black, anti-Hispanic, anti-Muslim, anti-you-name-it. He was a robe-wearing member of the KKK. He was a terrible landlord. In fact, Woodie Guthrie wrote a song about Fred called *Old Man Trump* in 1954:

I suppose that Old Man Trump knows just how
    much racial hate
He stirred up in that bloodpot of human hearts
When he drawed that color line
Here at his Beach Haven family project

Beach Haven ain't my home!
No, I just can't pay this rent!
My money's down the drain,
And my soul is badly bent!
Beach Haven is Trump's Tower
Where no black folks come to roam,
No, no, Old Man Trump!
Old Beach Haven ain't my home!
(Guthrie 1954)

"Probably, though, the most ironic thing about Fred and Donald is that Fred's father died in 1918, a victim of the Spanish Flu. He died from the worst pandemic in the world in the 20th century only to have his grandson screw up the COVID-19 pandemic response in the United States in the 21st. Let that sink in for a minute."

After a moment, I asked, "Can Fred ever complete his sentence?"

Arnold sadly shook his head. "Remember your Dante. There is no hope in Hell, there is no hope in Dante's *Inferno*, there is no hope in *Trump's Towering Inferno*. In Dante's theology, it's not the sins you commit that land you in Hell. It is the lack of contrition, of repentance, of simple self-knowledge. How can Fred complete a sentence he won't even acknowledge he deserves? You heard him deny all the evil activities he participated in. He not only was in New York City on the day of that KKK rally, he was there, in person, robed and ready to burn a cross. He'll never get out of here because he can't, or won't, acknowledge that what he did was wrong. It does not seem like he is going to change his tune. Until he does—if he does—he'll be here, with the U.S. Capitol police officers and every person setting foot into the building treading on Fred's head. It is a just and righteous punishment."

"May I ask you a question about that?"

"Ask away," said Arnold. "But I'll bet I know what's on your mind. You are wondering what the U.S. Capitol police officers are doing here, right?"

"Yes. I mean, are they doomed to Hell along with Fred Trump and the other enablers here? Some Capitol Police helped the January 6 insurrectionists, and I guess they deserve to be here, but they should be part of the flooring, themselves, not stepping on Trump.

"Remember that most of the beings here now are avatars. They represent real men and women who served in the U.S. Capitol Police on January 6, 2021, and they are honored here for their courage and bravery on that day.

"The Trump administration reflected so much irony, hypocrisy, and contradiction. Trump positioned himself as a law-and-order president. He supported police crackdowns on undocumented individuals in the United States. He wanted to send the National Guard in to suppress the Black Lives Matter protesters, most of whom were peaceful. He went on and on in his speeches about the importance of the police and how they were needed to Make America Great Again. And then he sent a crowd of domestic terrorists after them on January 6. Those yahoos attacked, beat, injured, maimed, and killed police officers. Trump orchestrated the greatest attack on the U.S. Capitol since the British burned it down during the War of 1812. These police officer avatars have been placed here and are pleased to establish authority and the rule of God's divine law here in *Trump's Towering Inferno*. We will see more of them as we move upward." He jerked his head in the direction of the escalator. "Let's move. Forward." Level two. Up the moving stairs. We'll visit your brothers of the quill there, the press. There we will see those who have dishonored that noble profession that was protected by the First Amendment. We will visit the liars, the provocateurs, the hypocrites, and fraudsters. They have their own level in *Trump's Towering Inferno*, and we'll go there next."

"Uhhh. You mean I must walk over the heads between here and there?"

"Yes, of course. Starting with Fred. Everyone steps on Fred. But don't think anything of it. He wouldn't hesitate for a minute to step on you, and neither would the others. Let's go."

"All right," I sighed. And I started across the lobby behind the general, stepping as lightly as possible.

Halfway toward the escalator, I stopped. There was what appeared to be a bowling ball sitting between the various heads just to my right.

"What's that" I asked.

"Ahhh," came his response. "That is Michael Cohen's spot."

"Where is he now?"

"I don't know, exactly. But he is being processed, I'm sure," said the general.

"What does that mean?"

"Well, Michael earned his spot here, that's for certain," the general said. "Cohen served as Trump's personal attorney for 12 years. Known as 'Trump's fixer,' he also served as vice-president of the Trump Organization and deputy finance chairman of the Republican National Committee, among other titles and positions.

"But" Arnold continued, "Michael is trying to make amends. He's trying to work his way out of Hell, step by step. I think it is unclear what his future holds. That's why the orb is in his place. If it is determined that Michael is not truly repentant, he'll be back in that space faster than you can say 'Bill Barr.'"

Next to the Cohen "orb" was another face I remembered from photos.

"Who is that?" I asked?

"That," replied the general, "is Roy Cohn. Trump's first 'fixer' and mentor. He represents all that is despised in lawyers, including lying, bullying, manipulating, and bribing governmental and business leaders. He is pond scum. He always found his way to the intersection of politics and the media. He came to national attention as a staff member of Joseph McCarthy during the 1950's, and learned that truth has little to do with perception in the political and public opinion worlds. Cohn once said:

"I don't want to know what the law is. I want to know who the judge is," he said of the cases he was working on. (Meacham 2018:206)

"Cohn worked with Roger Stone in the 1979–1980 presidential campaign of Ronald Reagan. It's like these bad apples keep showing up together and move from scandal to scandal, doing the dirty work so that the politicians and business leaders can get away with unethical and illegal activities.

"Roger Stone is somewhere here, too," Arnold stated flatly. "Another arsehole. His career is nothing but a string of immoral and illegal campaign activities for Republican candidates from Richard Nixon to Donald Trump. His political modus operandi has always been 'attack, attack, attack—never defend' and 'Admit nothing, deny everything, launch counterattack'" (Toobin 2008).

"These so-called 'fixers' aren't fixers at all—they are best described as 'breakers,' as in they break down society, the rule of law and democracy by bribing, bending, and breaking the letter and spirit of the law for money. They are legal mercenaries, following the flow of money from those they represent. Its attorneys like this that give the profession a bad rep."

As we moved forward again toward the escalator, I saw four U.S. Capitol police officers come into the lobby, move toward one of the heads jutting from the floor, and began removing him (I could clearly see it was a man but wasn't sure who it was).

"Who is that," I asked.

"That's Michael Lindell," the general replied.

"Who?"

"Michael Lindell. You might know him as 'My Pillow Guy.'"

"What are they doing with him?"

"He's being removed and sent to processing for future assignment."

"Really? Why? He's done great harm to our nation, spreading Trump's Big Lie about the 2020 election. He not only said that Trump won more than 80 million votes, but that the Chinese were involved and that the Democrats counted votes for dead people, nonresidents, minors, and more, as I recall."

"Well, yes, that's how he ended up here. He supported the 'Big Lie,' no doubt. His success and attempts to change the election were too high for his nut. But information collected by the Heavenly research department concluded that Michael does not belong here. While he used his wealth to spread 'The Big Lie,' he did it out of ignorance, not malice. The others you will see here in *Trump's Towering Inferno* conducted their business and support of Trump out of malice. Turns out Michael is really stupid, and really gullible. He believes Trump actually won," the general stated, a wry smile on his face. "He also believes that the January 6 protesters were peaceful, kind, and loving. What a moron."

"So, that gets him a free pass out of *Inferno*?" I asked.

"Well, at least for now. You see, intentions matter. Those you will find here were condemned because they knowingly committed crimes against humanity. They supported the Great Traitor despite knowing what he was doing was wrong. You cannot claim ignorance of the law in the United States as a defense for breaking the law, but here ignorance is considered. You won't see Trumpers here who believed Trump was Making America Great Again. You will see those who knowingly participated in his evil activities, from his businesses to his campaign and presidency. Michael Lindell is stupid. The Almighty understands that, and he'll be processed to a more appropriate location."

I frowned. "I thought he must be smart," I said. "Hasn't he

made millions through his pillow sales business?"

"Well, he did make millions. He had one clever idea and was good at promoting it. I mean, look at his face. He's an affable, believable type of guy. By hugging his pillow and calling himself 'My Pillow Guy,' he seemed to have been at the right place at the right time. But really his pillows were no better than anyone else's. He was a shoddyocracy—a seller of overpriced merchandise. He's more lucky than smart."

We continued, reaching the escalator a moment later.

Halfway up the escalator, I heard a commotion at the door and looked over my shoulder. The Capitol police officers were dragging an old man, kicking, and screaming, toward an elevator.

"Who is that?" I asked.

"That's Josh Hawley."

"He certainly didn't age well." The guards had little problem dragging the old man across the room and seemed to take extra pleasure in roughing him up a bit. "Where is he going?"

"He's just been processed. Although he lived a long life, after his failed attempts at the presidency, his life spiraled downward. He was fired after a brief stint at the Fox network, then found himself homeless after his divorce and bankruptcy hearing. He lived on government welfare until he became eligible for his pension and Social Security, but with so much of it owed to creditors from the court cases and lawsuits he lost, he could not move out of the low-income, government-built housing projects. In other words, he was forced to rely on safety net programs he tried hard to eliminate." A ghost of a smile played on the General's lips.

"We'll see him again when he has been assigned his "forever home."

I was happy to be leaving the lobby.

CHAPTER 2

SECOND FLOOR: MANIPULATORS OF THE MASSES

There once was an old man who lived in a tower,
Not happy with life, he craved more power.
He lied and he cheated and he bullied his foes.
His treasonous ways have now been exposed.

The general stepped cautiously off the escalator, like children and the elderly often do. I glanced at him quizzically. He caught my eyes.

"I'm adjusting," he explained. "Moving staircases, horseless carriages, flying stagecoaches, images of people and items displayed in boxes and on walls and that inner-net thing (I assumed he meant the Internet—I saw no point in correcting him). It's a lot to take in. Your America has come so far, with your technical advances, but your morality . . . well, not so much. I'm not saying we were all saints in our day. We had our vanity and false gods. But we never worshipped wealth like you all do. You don't care for the poor and destitute. You begrudge every cent it costs to keep a person with few options alive. In a land of great resources and financial wealth, you allow a small number of families to control most of the nation's wealth and resources while millions live in poverty and children go to bed hungry. You elected a con man as your president. You cheered while he flaunted the money he "earned" off the backs of the underserved tenants and then placed other rich white men in positions of power, many of whom had also gotten rich by dishonest and illegal means.

"Then they passed laws and created policies that allowed the rich to make even more money and paid the most vulnerable even less. They passed tax cuts for the wealthy and allowed the richest Americans and corporations to avoid taxes just as Trump, his father, and family have done for decades. Absolutely amazing!"

You know, I fought in both the French and Indian wars, and the War for Independence. We fought for ideals, not loot, and considered war a last resort. It was never a way of life for us. In fact, the United States disbanded our Navy in 1781 and had none until 1794. You're no longer fighting in Central Asia, but your war budget is still larger than the rest of the world's combined and keeps climbing! The resources you spend to fund a full-time war-making machine could fund a decent standard of living for everyone, not only in the United States but all over the planet."

"It's not that simple . . ." I began.

"Yes, it is," Arnold snapped. "Wars are rarely fought by armies, these days. They're insurgencies. Standing armies and navies are no defense against insurgencies, so why maintain them? Shift your resources from weapons of death and destruction to an arsenal of life-sustaining projects such as food, shelter, education, and health care. There's never going to be another Battle of Midway. Do you think Al Qaeda or ISIS care how many aircraft carriers you have? Why not try gradually reducing U.S. military spending while increasing foreign aid, and see if that doesn't make you allies around the world who you won't need a massive military to defend yourself against? Why not try 'beating your swords into plowshares and spears into pruning hooks,' or, in contemporary terms, convert your rifles into rakes and transform your tanks into tractors? The United States is more powerful than any nation or empire in history. You still could create and maintain a *Pax Americana*. Your dominance around the world in military, economic, and cultural areas invites—I stand corrected, *demands*—your leadership to solve pressing global concerns. Instead, you continue to prepare for and engage in wars to solve international conflict. My old colleague and friend, then enemy, General Washington, warned you to stay away from foreign entanglements, but you have ignored his advice. Your military budget is unsustainable, counterproductive, and immoral. Unless you change your ways, your time at the top will soon come to an end."

We moved away from the escalator and into the second floor. We approached a hallway that ended at the top of what looked like a midsized basketball arena. In the center of the room, instead of a basketball court, five large, flat-screen televisions faced different directions around the room. Each television was about 10 feet wide and six or seven feet tall. Their sides came together, and they created a pentagonal shape.

I also saw rows of individuals seated around the room at different levels, moving up from the center where the large televisions were located toward the top, where the general and I stood. The first level had one person sitting in front of each television, or five individuals total. At each level, there were more individuals. I observed 10 persons on the second level, two watching the screen in front of them, then 15 on the third level, where three were looking at the screen in front of them, and so forth, up through nine levels. I estimated there were about 250 individuals in this room, with more on each level as they moved further up and away from the central bank of televisions.

The televisions were tuned to different news channels. I could readily make out the logos as I walked around the room: CNN, MSNBC, CBS, ABC, and PBS.

"What is this?" I asked.

"This is the second level of *Trump's Towering Inferno*, a level devoted to the liars and manipulators of truth who broadcast their message of hatred and animosity across the airwaves, as you call them, and were watched and listened to in millions of homes across America.

"It is one thing," he continued, "to have and share your own opinion. Everyone has an opinion. You are free to share your opinion. You can also be wrong. Everyone is wrong and makes mistakes. To err is human, as you know.

"But these people intentionally distorted information. They are peddlers of disinformation. I was sometimes wrong in what I believed to be true. I made mistakes. When I learned the truth, I gave up my previous position.

"These men and women herein placed by the Divine Judge were not just wrong about what they said. They deliberately and purposefully told lies and falsehoods. They used their positions to spew hatred, racism, and other forms of disinformation intentionally to those who watched them on TV. Therefore, they have been placed on the second level of *Trump's Towering Inferno*."

We walked down the steps toward the center of the room. There was a row of five individuals directly in front of the large screen television, looking up at it as if they had been seated in the front row of a movie theater. I saw the back of the heads of these five individuals, who were securely strapped onto their hard, wooden seats.

"Do I know these four men and one woman?" I asked.

"Maybe," came his reply. "They are the worst of the worst. This group had the greatest negative impact on the United

States based on a formula that measured the size of their audience and their level of lying and disinformation. They are Rush Limbaugh, Rupert Murdoch, Laura Ingraham, Sean Hannity, and Tucker Carlson.

"Like the others in this room, they spread the lies that led to Trump's ascension to the White House, among many other misdeeds. Tucker's later campaigns for the presidency created its own pain across the nation. These five were supporters of the 'Birther Movement,' the crazy, racist campaign that sought to delegitimize the presidency of Barack Obama by insisting that he was not a born in the United States. Further, the Birther Movement, by trying to spread the lie that Obama was not a citizen of the United States, stoked the deep-seated racism that goes back to the colonial period in which African men and women were enslaved and the First Settlers became victims of a genocidal campaign.

"This foul group knew better. They knew Obama was born in Hawaii *after* it became a state. But they were racists and opportunists. There was no barrier too low for them to go under in their quest for personal fame and fortune.

"There was once a day when newspaper reporters and radio and TV news broadcasters sought the truth. Theirs was an honorable trade and ethical profession. It is true that reporters and anchors like Edward E Murrow, Walter Cronkite, Tom Brokaw, Peter Jennings, Chet Huntley, and David Brinkley, for instance, made mistakes. But they did not deliberately mislead the American public. They never told bald-faced lies during their broadcast or reporting careers.

"But Limbaugh, Murdoch, Ingraham, Hannity, and Carlson were heinous, vile, revolting individuals who easily qualified for a place in *Trump's Towering Inferno*. Their distortions and deformations, deception and dishonesty, their falsehoods and fabrications to nation-wide audiences put them head and shoulders above the rest. They created a new form of dishonesty and hatred that had negative consequences for the immediate and long-range future of democracy and decency in the United States and around the world. They could all tell a thumper, that's for sure."

"Can I speak to them?" I asked.

"You can speak to them, but they won't speak back."

"Really? Why not?"

"You'll see."

I walked over to the spot where Rush Limbaugh was sitting. His eyes were fixed on the screen in front of him. It was a live broadcast of MSNBC's The Rachel Maddow Show. Belts, chains, and shackles held his face and gaze in place. His face was red, the veins of his neck were swollen, his eyes bulged out. I've seen angry men and women before—Limbaugh was fuming.

"Greetings, Mr. Limbaugh. Can I ask you a few questions?"

Painfully, slowly, he turned against the restraints toward me and shrugged his shoulders.

"I guess I have two questions. How are you, and why are you here?"

He opened his mouth and tried to talk, but all that came out was guttural mumblings and an incoherent noise. Reddening more, he tried again, but with the same results, albeit it a bit louder. After a few minutes, I asked the general what the problem was.

"He can't talk. No one in this room can speak anymore. This is their punishment. They who lied and spread misinformation for so long can't communicate with anyone. They are fixed here, watching the news, unable to speak or connect to other human beings."

"Really," I muttered. "Why?"

"They've had their tongues cut out. They try to talk but are only capable of making primitive sounds. To be truthful, the sounds they make now are harmless. After decades of lies and spewing anger and hate, they are, for all intents and purposes, silenced at last.

"Think of the damage they did while alive. Rush's broadcasts stoked the flames of racism, homophobia, antifeminism, and the denial of climate change. He got behind Trump even though Trump's policies and agenda were anything but what conservative Republicans, which Limbaugh claimed to support, stood for.

"Rush was like a John the Baptist for the new right-wing media that has expanded now to Alt-Right. He was the first to discover that he could make millions by speaking to the anger and resentments of many white Americans. The hatred he emitted gave birth to a whole new industry: hate radio."

Arnold kicked at the dirt and shook his head, then continued.

"Rush himself was a hypocrite and liar on so many fronts. Family values, drug addiction, honesty. It's no wonder that he and Trump got along because Rush has also been found guilty of the cardinal sins, yes? Lust, check. Gluttony, check. Greed, check. Wrath, check. Envy, check. Pride, check. The only thing you could say he did not exhibit in his life was slothfulness. In reality, he would have done less harm had he been as intellectually and personally lazy as Trump. But, like Trump, the two were walking exemplars of most sins."

"What about the others?"

"Same shit, different arseholes," he replied. "Go ahead. Speak to Rupert, Laura, Sean, or Tucker. You'll get the same response. It's difficult to say who was the worst of these celebrity fibbers. Maybe Rush because he showed the way. But once the door was open, they all crawled out of their roach motels and achieved fame and fortune through their lies and distortions of truth. Take Ruppert, for instance. He was an international press tycoon, a seller, and maker, of the news. In England, for example, where Prime Minister Boris Johnson, another windbag / mini-Trump, urged his people to get the COVID-19 vaccine, Murdoch's newspapers encouraged its readers to follow his advice. At the same time, Trump and his Republican allies in the United States cast doubt on the threat of COVID-19 and the efficacy of the vaccine. Murdoch's news media in the United States deplored the same vaccine and doubted its safety and effectiveness. He was Machiavellian—working both sides of the same issue to increase his personal wealth and fortune, as well as his power and influence in these and other nations.

"Or Tucker. Tuck has built an empire through a steady stream of bold lying coupled with racism and sexism. He promotes conspiracy theories such as the Great White Replacement Theory. Here's the reality: the Great White Replacement Theory came into existence only as a conspiracy theory. There is no organized effort to replace white persons in the U.S. None. He denied the dangers of COVID-19, scorned the mask mandates and social distancing and actively scared his followers away from life-saving vaccines. He denies Global Climate Change, casts doubt on the intentions of the Black Lives Matter protestors, and claimed in, 2021 that 'there was no physical evidence that George Floyd was murdered by a cop' and 'the autopsy showed that

Tucker Carlson

George Floyd almost certainly died of a drug overdose.' He called Supreme Court nominee Ketanji Brown Jackson 'ignorant of the law' and said her place on the court would 'defile, humiliate and degrade the court's effectiveness.' He is a supporter of the Big Lie and said that 'there's no evidence that white supremacists were responsible for what happened on January 6th. That's a lie.' Further, he has promoted one of the conspiracy theories that the January 6 attack was a false flag FBI operation designed to 'suppress political dissent.' WTF."

"So, it's a waste of time to speak to them," I concluded.

"I would think so."

"Two more questions for you, then," I said.

"Go ahead."

"Okay. First, is this a just punishment for them? It seems soft compared to the men and women we saw on the first floor who will be stepped on for eternity. They are suffering the steps and kicks of the Capitol Hill police officers and every other visitor to *Trump's Towering Inferno*. Isn't that worse?"

"Think this through for yourself," he said. "Consider this: these individuals, each who made their names through the news industry, who impacted the opinion of millions of men and women in the United States and around the world, are now silenced forever. They thrived on attention their entire lives. The higher they climbed, the larger their audience, the bigger their lies. Their punishment is an eternity of watching the news reported by men and women who share the news with truth and honesty. They will watch some men and women who have progressive worldviews, and others with traditional worldviews. They will watch men and women who do their best to deliver the news in an objective manner.

"Those sentenced here will have to watch the mainstream networks and cable shows with the highest integrity in ethics ratings. CBS, ABC, NBC, PBS, CNN, MSNBC. These are not 'fake news outlets.' Sure, they make mistakes now and again, and sometimes the mistakes are whoppers, or they get the story completely wrong. But they try to tell the truth, at least, most of the time. And, when they make mistakes, they own them. You can't say that about those in this room."

From time to time, I saw the news on each television change to a different channel and different news report. Every row of individuals saw the same show, but the different televisions showed different channels and different broadcasts to those watching. As the channels changed, I could see that each row was getting essentially the same information on the same story, just from different, independent broadcasters.

"These men and women being punished on this level can't interrupt, respond, or spin their far-flung conspiracy plots.

"Finally, they are cut off from each other, their audiences, humanity, and the divine. Their punishment is to sit for eternity watching others give the news while they have no ability to talk. In my opinion, this will torment these men and women more than any physical ailment."

"Point taken," I said.

"Your other question," the general asked.

"Yes. I see the logos of prominent television networks. But I don't see Fox anywhere around the room. Am I just missing their broadcasts?"

Arnold fixed me with a hard stare.

"There was a day when it might have been permissible to show Fox here. But at this point, no one has any patience for their bollocks. Fox is nothing more than a propaganda outlet. They do little more than promote talking points for specific candidates and their right-wing conspiracy theories. We are aware of the hatred and misinformation they are spreading—and there will be justice. But we don't have time to watch that channel here."

"So, the other men and women in this room?"

"Other lying, self-serving radio and television broadcasters from the United States and around the world. They did not reach the fame and power of the Big Five in the middle of the room, but they sold the same lies, and their punishment is identical. Tongues cut out. Eternity watching other networks. Alone forever.

"In the second row we have those whose ambition and ethical shortcomings drove them to near the top of their profession. Each circle shows men and women with a diminishing impact, because they were in smaller markets or had fewer viewers, often because they were not as popular, talented, attractive, charismatic, or capable of lying with as much audacity as those in the levels below them.

"These men and women were fearmongers. They demonized Democrats and progressives and advanced the idea of 'owning the libs.' They got doses of the COVID-19 vaccines as quickly as they could but would not tell whether they had received their vaccines to their audiences and often discouraged these same viewers from getting vaccines. That's called hypocrisy. In fact, many of them promoted the horse deworming medicine Ivermectin and other useless snake oil as cures for COVID. Do you think any of them took Ivermectin? Of course not. More hypocrisy.

"They invited quacks and fringe medical personnel onto their shows to question the true science and research being conducted at the highest levels of universities and governments. They contributed to the ongoing pandemic and made it worse. But by 2022, more men and women living in Red States, or Republican-leaning states, were infected or died from COVID than those in Blue States. Like sheep being led to the slaughter, they followed their political and TV personalities right to the grave."

He paused again, scratched his head, and tried to refocus.

"In the second row, for instance, you have Bill O'Reilly, Lou Dobbs, Ben Shapiro, Candance Owens, Glenn Beck, Eric Bolling, Steve Doocy, Gretchen Carlson, Brian Kilmeade, and Ainsley Earhardt. These 10 form the second tier of the manipulators of the masses, the men and women who used hatred and disinformation for personal and political gain. Behind them are more and more television and radio personalities ascending upward. They are all forced to watch the real news and unable to speak or communicate with anyone else.

"They are also traitors to the United States of America. Like Trump, they promoted their own interests over the interests of the United States. They supported The Big Lie. They stood behind the traitor Trump. They helped divide this great nation. They were traitors, wrapping themselves in the flag while actively tearing it to shreds."

"I pity them," I said. It was true.

"This is indeed a terrible way to spend eternity," the General sighed. "But step back from your pity and acknowledge the pain and suffering they caused to others while on earth. Think of the decades the United States lost in not addressing global climate change, for instance. Think of the environmental degradation, mass extinction of species, and the death of the Amazon rainforest and boreal forests of Siberia and North America. Further, the acidification of the oceans, pollution of fresh water in streams and ponds. A move to green technology decades earlier would have created jobs and mitigated the impact of humans on this planet. They were racists pigs, Trump acolytes. They were as responsible for the million deaths from COVID-19 as the Liar in Chief. Let them rot here and put them out of your mind."

"Um, all right. What's next?"

"The next level, of course," he replied. "We'll take the stairs."

THIRD FLOOR: THE CHRISTIAN WRONGS

The Donald is my shepherd, I follow no other.
He makes me lie down in his bed of lies;
    he leads me through stormy waters;
    he taketh my soul.
He leads me in the wrong path
  for personal glory.

Even though I walk through the darkest valley,
    I fear no evil;
for the Republican governors and members of
Congress are with me.
Your rod and your balls
They help me to cope.

You prepare a table before me
In the presence of other hypocrites.
You bless my bank account with money
My wallet overflows.

Surely greed and corruption shall follow me
All the days of my life
And I will dwell in *Trump's Towering Inferno*
For ever more.

We reached the third floor. I was hoping the journey might get easier emotionally, mentally, physically, and spiritually, but I could now see that was not going to happen. I thought back to Trump's presidency. What struck me was not that so many despicable individuals found themselves in his administration. What was truly remarkable was that there were so many despicable people in the United States. During the campaign of 2016, Hillary Clinton had to walk back her statement that half of Trump's supporters were "a basket of deplorables." But had she said his inner circle were these deplorables, she would have been spot on. They *are*, with few exceptions, a group of "racist, sexist, homophobic, xenophobic, Islamophobic" men and women.

As the door at the top of the staircase opened, I saw what appeared to be—could it really be? —a gladiator arena. We came into a room that rang with screams of pain and terror. The room was split in half. There were men and women, dressed in ragged, ripped, and tattered suits and dresses to our right, with another group of men and women, dressed in jeans, sweatpants, and tee-shirts on the left.

Those dressed in the frayed and shredded clothing, to my right, were bleeding from head to foot, bruised, battered, beaten, and broken. I thought of the photos and videos I have seen of war victims, fleeing the bombed cities and villages where they had lived. I thought of the orphans I work with in sub-Saharan Africa. They all have that same look.

Further, these men and women were moving in slow motion, like they had large weights on their backs or were walking in deep mud, as in one of my recurring dreams where I am trying to run but can't get up to speed. My legs won't respond, and I can't do what I know I can do. That's what was happening to these men and women.

Then, something startling took place. One of the men on my left picked up a baseball-sized rock, ran to the middle of the room, and threw it toward one of the men on my right. The rock hit him on his temple, just above his left eye. The blow staggered the man, but he did not go down. Fresh blood came pouring out of his wound, which began to swell.

I then saw dozens of men and women throwing stones. Some struck the men and women standing in the first row, while other stones flew over the heads of this first group and hit others standing behind. There must have been 100 to 200 men and women dressed in the shredded clothing, with another 500 on my left picking up and throwing rocks. It was a scene you could not make up.

"What the . . ." I stammered.

"This is third level of *Trump's Towering Inferno*. This one is reserved for the sheep in wolf's clothing, the religious leaders, the men, and women who sold their souls for fame and fortune by supporting the most immoral man to hold the presidency in U.S. history. And to call Trump the most immoral man to hold the presidency is saying a lot!

"It is bad enough," the general continued, "to lie and cheat and take advantage of others for your own personal fame and fortune. Millions of businessmen and women do that all the time to increase their profits. But it is especially reprehensible to invoke God's name to fleece your flock for personal wealth. These men and women to our right used religion and cited scriptural passages to seduce members of their churches to donate resources that these charlatans took for personal gain. Many naïve and gullible individuals, often at vulnerable times in their lives, gave these swindlers their resources, sometimes sinking themselves into poverty. Their donations were not used as they wanted them to be, or maybe only a fraction of what they gave was used that way, but many of their hard-earned donations ended up enabling these clergy to live in wealth and luxury. Those who were promised physical healing did not receive physical healing.

Those promised they would gain material wealth on this planet if they sacrificed and gave generously to these sharks did not gain wealth and prosperity. They were conned."

"And these are Christian clergy?"

"NO! They are not," Arnold shouted, thrusting his index finger in my direction as an impassioned preacher might have. "They are low-life, bottom-dwelling scum who *portrayed* themselves as Christian ministers. They pretended to be pious, holy, and faithful clergymen and clergywomen. Sure, some had official status and denominational credentials, but others were self-declared and self-ordained, with little or no theological training or education. Most claimed to be evangelical and members of the so-called Christian Right, but they preached a message far from the Gospel message of Jesus Christ. They should be called the Christian Wrongs. They are reviled and scorned by the saints on earth and in Heaven. They give many good, kind, humble, and faithful clergy a bad name, and have turned millions away from faith and churches within the United States."

"You know I'm ordained, right?"

"Of course. But you seem to be a man of the cloth who's cut from a different bolt of cloth, at least you're different from these yahoos. I will say this for them. They were often shrewd. They were tech-savvy and could act. They would cry and then turn toward the television camera or audience and beg for money like their lives depended on it. Oh, they are good at raising money, but not so good at serving God or using those funds for what their followers believed their gifts would be used for.

"And let me be perfectly clear," he continued. "There is nothing wrong or evil about collecting a salary as a man or woman of the cloth. Clergy should have salaries, housing, health care, and pensions. But those living in million-dollar homes, driving luxury cars, wearing expensive designer clothing and jewelry . . . Come on."

Arnold paused again. He breathed deeply. Although he was striving to be a dispassionate and objective guide, he was warming emotionally in a way he did not want. He rubbed his eyes and continued.

"Now, it was not evil to have been a Christian and voted for Donald Trump in 2016 or 2020. Millions of Christians did just that. Nor was it evil to be a clergy member and have pulled the lever for Donald Trump. Thousands of clergy did that as well.

"Trump did appoint judges to the court who were pro-life, making his Christian Right base happy. He spoke at churches and courted these and other church leaders. He quoted, or attempted to quote, from the Bible. Some Christians accepted him as a work in progress. Fine. Others thought he was God's special envoy. While we found that inexplicable, it is true there were well-meaning and well-intentioned clergy and laity who voted for Donald Trump and viewed him as a savior to Christianity.

"What was unacceptable was the clergy using their positions and power to endorse and campaign for Mr. Trump. To stand by his side at his events and rallies and to bring him into their 'houses of worship.' Further, to say he was a 'gift from God,' or 'God's chosen servant,' or 'God's messenger.' We understand that many of these men and women supported Trump because of his position on abortion, which, conveniently, Trump changed in time for the 2016 election. But to worship at his feet, to suggest that it was God's will that he was elected? To claim that anyone who opposed Trump's agenda opposed God's agenda? These claims were inexcusable and baseless.

"The reporter Sarah Posner said it well, and I paraphrase her when I say that these people before you defended Trump from criticism as men and women of 'the cloth.' Because they were clergy, they gave cover to his racism and white nationalism. They excused and rationalized his tweets and statements and claimed they were misunderstood or manipulated by the 'fake news,' designed to make Trump look bad. They blamed Trump critics for creating divisions, when in reality it was Trump and his evangelical base that moved us toward this unthinkable reality: the United States had an overtly racist president" (Posner, 2020: 37).

"It turns out that many in the Christian Right *are* racists themselves, and when their supporters and church members see these church leaders making racists statements, it strengthens the racism of other Americans who also see themselves as Christians."

I admitted, "I never had much time, or interest, watching the televangelists, nor the clergy of the megachurches of the Christian Right. I don't recognize them. Who are they?"

"As you can see, they are spread out in rows, with the worst offenders toward the front, then moving backwards toward those who had similar worldviews behind stretching to the back of the room.

"Again, the 'worst' is a bit subjective, but is based on the individual's perversion of the Christian gospel mixed with the size of their church or television audience and negative impact they had. Believe me, there are many who fleeced their congregations, who lived in million-dollar houses, who spread hatred, division, and bigotry. Those you see here, though, were the worst of the lot."

"Let me be crystal clear: The messages of these 'ministers' is as far from authentic Christianity as possible. Theirs is *not* a message of grace and peace, mercy, and love. They do not preach self-sacrifice or take up their crosses to follow Jesus. Instead, they riffed on Old Testament themes. They were vengeful. Angry. Judgmental. They echoed and stoked the culture wars. They were anti-LGBT. Anti-immigrant. Anti-Muslim. Against the poor and downtrodden. They were, in a word, anti-Christs.

"What they stood for," he continued, "sadly and ironically, was wealth, power, domination, and authority. Jesus was a Mediterranean peasant who said 'blessed are you who are poor,' and 'woe to you who are rich' (NRSV, 1991; Luke 6:20, 24). Yet these men and women preached a message called the Prosperity Gospel that emphasized material riches over spiritual ones. They did not focus on service to the poor but on personal wealth. They told their followers that if they gave them and their ministries money, those individuals themselves would be blessed with raises and promotions or be healed from any and all disease."

"That message is nothing new," I said. "It's no better or worse than what the Catholics used to do by selling indulgences, the concept that you could get your relatives out of Hell by making a donation to the church. Humans can't control God. Not then, not now."

"Seriously," said Arnold, "are you excusing these wolves in sheep's' clothing? Trying to see the best? It's not there to be seen! Jesus brought a message of peace and love. These men and women supported war and the military-industrial-political complex. Jerry Falwell, Sr., placed here in the second tier of Christian Wrongs, once wrote a tract called *God is*

Pro-War (Jerry Falwell, 2004). "There is nothing in the gospels that can be used or twisted to a message of hatred, violence, or war. Jesus was one of the great pacifists of all time." (Brown 1985) "A church or a Christian that does not take a stand against war is a Christian or church that does not deserve to be believed." (Cox 1965)

"In addition, they pledged their unfailing faith in and support for Donald Trump. They compared Trump to Jesus Christ himself, and King Cyrus, from the Old Testament, who freed the Jews from bondage to end the Babylonian Captivity. When Trump declared that he had done more for Christianity than Jesus himself, they applauded and agreed with him.

"Trump's declaration of doing more for Christianity than anyone else is blasphemy! And yet they endorsed and supported him.

"They were total arseholes. Wolves in sheep's clothing. Their support of Trump gave him a false appearance of spiritual support or blessing, which allowed many who should have known better to be sucked into this orbit and support him.

"The Bible is filled with warning against false teachers, from the earliest writings of the Old Testament through the Book of Revelation. Jesus himself addressed this many times, including in his Sermon on the Mount, where he said:

> Not everyone who says to me, 'Lord, Lord,'
> will enter the kingdom of Heaven, but only
> the one who does the will of my Father
> in Heaven. On that day many will say to
> me, 'Lord, Lord, did we not prophesy in
> your name, and cast out demons in your
> name, and do many deeds of power in your

name?' Then I will declare to them, 'I never knew you; go away from me, you evildoers.'
(NRSV, 1991; Matthew 7:21–23)

"Yet, sadly, many have believed and followed false prophets through the centuries. In every age, liars take advantage of good-hearted, easy-to-fleece individuals who trust them. Those in front of us not only hustled their own people, but they also helped lift Trump up to the presidency.

"They threw stones at others their whole lives and ministries. As I just said, they verbally attacked Muslims, Jews, progressive Christians, and members of post-Christian organizations. They went after the LGBT community. They attacked politicians in the center and those on the left with whom they disagreed. They used their positions not only to become extraordinarily wealthy but also to convince their adherents that they should cast their votes for Trump. Donald Trump would not have won the presidency in 2016 without the support of these Christian Wrongs.

"Their punishment is simple. They will be stoned for eternity. They who publicly supported Trump and helped build the myth that he was chosen by God to lead the United States will be struck by stones from now until the end of time. Although they often, falsely, claimed to have been persecuted in life and compared themselves to the early Christians who were truly persecuted and punished and literally thrown to the lions and gladiators in the Roman coliseums, these self-serving clergy have earned a just punishment. They will be stoned, but never die. They will be hit, but not killed. They will bleed, they will bruise, and they will suffer. This is their place in Hell."

He went silent.

"Who are they?" I asked. "The ones throwing the rocks?"

"Ah," he said. "Those are the men and women who were conned out of their money. You'll see good, salt-of-the-earth men and women who believed what they heard from this scum. The men and women you see throwing the stones believed that if they gave money to their ministries, they would receive more than they gave, or their cancers would be cured, or God would bless them or impart special privileges to the United States.

"They are, of course, like the U.S. Capitol police officers. They are not real people, but avatars of those individuals who supported these charlatans.

"There is the avatar of a woman who gave her entire savings, $14,000, and most of her pension, only to end up homeless. Another couple who sold their home and donated the proceeds to one of these arseholes but instead of reaping God's blessings, her donations, along with those of other swindled men and women, enabled that false prophet to purchase a multi-million-dollar home. Naive high school and college students were hustled out of room, board, and tuition payments they had saved for their college education. And there are many, many more stories like theirs."

I had all the information I needed to understand the activity of this floor, but I had a few more questions. How do you approach men and women being stoned? Or the people stoning them? What's the right thing to say to either party? Words of comfort? Should I ask about regrets? Would they do it all again?

"You will be safe," the general said, as if reading my mind. "Those stones will not hit you."

Still, I hesitated, and not only for fear of being hit by one of the stones. How much did I really want to know about these pelted pastors and clobbered clergy? Who, other than a hard-nosed journalist, would want to know the thoughts of those being tormented?

But I was brought here for a reason. Pulling up my big boy pants, I moved toward the front row. I spent an hour among the denizens on this floor of Hell, and true to Arnold's word, was not so much as grazed by the stones that regularly sailed past. During that hour, I approached and spoke to six individuals nearest the jeering mob, as if in the front row. Others cowered and moaned behind them, themselves the targets of flying missiles.

Here is what I learned:

Though all were clothed in tatters, they once had been fashionably dressed. In fact, the remnants of men's suits had once been finely tailored designer products of Armani, Burberry, Gucci, and Cuccinelli. One woman wore a ripped and stained garment that had been an Oscar de la Renta sheath dress, while another was dressed from head to toe in bits of a torn Michael Kors outfit. Certainly, these persons had possessed great wealth before they were confined here in the third level of *Trump's Towering Inferno*. They had gone from riches to rags.

I learned their names and, like my other conversations I had in *Trump's Towering Inferno*, I discovered that they had no remorse, regret, or shame for what they had done during their time on earth. They blamed the press and others whom they described as petty, jealous and persons of no faith determined to hurt their ministries. They argued that they were innocent, had done nothing wrong, should not have been sentenced to this punishment, and believed that one day their "appeals" would be heard. On that day when their appeals were judged, they predicted they would win their cases and be brought straight to Heaven and seated by Jesus's side in the front row of a Trump MAGA rally. Their delusions saddened me, but I could find in my heart no sympathy for them.

Here are some of the clergy I interviewed:

- **Franklin Graham**. Graham's story is a sad tale of promise and potential for good taking a hard and tragic turn. The son of Billy Graham, Franklin had big shoes to fill and could have used his position as the president and CEO of the Billy Graham Evangelistic Association and of Samaritan's Purse, an international Christian relief agency, to do great things. In fact, those organizations did *some* great work and good deeds. But they could, and should have, done more. Franklin fell victim to his own greed, taking $1.2 million in compensation in 2008 and more extravagant compensation later. Franklin also fell victim to his pride and prejudice, using his high-profile position to criticize Islam, saying in 2001 (after the terrorist attacks on 9/11) that Islam is "a very evil and wicked religion," and in 2010, stating that Islam "is a religion of hatred. It's a religion of war." Further, Franklin, who supported Trump's candidacy for the presidency, commented on Facebook after the election that "God showed up. None of the so-called experts understood the God-factor." After 2016, Franklin remained one of the most vociferous, dogmatic allies of Trump. He suggested opposition to Trump was the work of a "demonic power" and in December 2020 wrote on Facebook that "President Trump will go down in history as one of the great presidents of our nation, bringing peace and prosperity to millions here in the U.S. and around the world."

- **Jerry Falwell Jr.** Like Franklin Graham, Jerry Falwell Jr. is the namesake son of a famous pastor. Falwell Sr. was, among other things, an American Southern Baptist pastor, televangelist, and conservative activist. He was the founder of Liberty University and the Moral Majority (which was neither moral nor held a majority of Americans in its worldview). In addition, as mentioned above, he was the author the essay "God is Pro-War" (Jerry Falwell, 2004). At a different time, in similar circumstances, he said, "It is the responsibility of every political conservative, every evangelical Christian, every prolife Catholic, every traditional Jew . . . to get serious about re-electing President [George W.] Bush" (*New York Times*, July 16, 2004). Jerry Sr. is now suffering for his own crimes against God and humanity.

Jerry Falwell Jr. is a chip off the old block. Junior attended Liberty University, then earned a law degree at the University of Virginia. He practiced law for 20 years, including serving as the lawyer for Liberty University and its related organizations. In 2007, on the death of his father, he became the president of Liberty University.

Although he was never ordained, he was one of the most prominent members of the evangelical Christian community and was seen by many as a religious leader. Like the others here in the third level of *Trump's Towering Inferno*, he:

- Made numerous disparaging remarks about members of the LGBT community, Muslims, Democrats, and others.

- Endorsed Donald Trump for the presidency on January 26, 2016, although it was later revealed that Michael Cohen had helped Junior recover some "compromising" photos of Junior's wife in exchange for the endorsement.

- Spoke in favor of Trump's candidacy at the Republican National Convention in 2016.

- In an August 2016 editorial in *The Washington Post*, he compared Trump to Winston Churchill.

- Shrugged off post-2016 election criticism from a group called the Red-Letter Christians that criticized Junior for his work in "forging the alliance between white evangelicals and Donald J. Trump, who won 81 percent of their vote."

- Invited Trump to speak at the graduation ceremony at Liberty University in 2017.

- Defended the president following his comments regarding the white supremacy attack in Charlottesville, Virginia, saying that the president does not have "a racist bone in his body."

- Answered this question in a January 2019: "Is there anything President Trump could do that would endanger that support from you or other evangelical leaders?" with one word: "No."

In addition to his unflagging support for Donald Trump, Junior was a vehement denier of COVID-19. He fought to keep Liberty University open despite criticism from the governor of Virginia (Ralph Northam), the mayor of Lynchburg (Treney Tweedy), professors, and the university's lead physician, Dr. Thomas Eppes, Jr. He promoted a conspiracy theory that the North Korean and Chinese governments had created the virus and blamed the press for exaggerating the dangers of COVID-19, saying, "They are willing to destroy the economy just to hurt Trump."

Finally, like Trump, Junior is a sexual deviant. At Liberty University, he showed sexually provocative photos of his wife to colleagues and shared a photo on Instagram of himself with his jeans unzipped and his arm around a young woman whose jeans were also unzipped. Junior was holding a glass with a dark drink within. And then, the biggest bombshell of all—Junior resigned as president of Liberty University after it was revealed that his wife had an ongoing, long-time affair with a pool attendant they met in 2012, and that Junior had often watched their lovemaking, either in person or on video.

So, it is okay, more or less, to be a sexual deviant. Most of us believe that what you do in the privacy of your bedroom is your own business, as long as everyone involved is a consenting adult and no one is being hurt through exploitation, sexual assault, or rape. But here is where hypocrisy and karma meet. If you stand in an ivory tower and throw stones at others for their moral behavior, and you behave in a similar, or worse manner, you lose your credibility and authority.

Junior walked away from Liberty University with a $10.5 million severance package. Now, he is trying to dodge, in slow motion, stones thrown by angry men and women whose money he and the others received in compensation for their "religious work." He is harvesting what he planted.

- **Paula White.** No one should be surprised that I encountered Paula White here, placed in the middle of the front row: after all, she was the woman known as Trump's spiritual advisor. Her coiffed hair, makeup, and jewelry were absent. Instead, I approached a woman battered beyond recognition. Her face was covered with scars and fresh wounds. Her Oscar de la Renta dress was shredded and covered in blood. She was barefoot, her patent leather stilettos gone. She was also moving slowly, unable to dodge the incoming stones aimed carefully and deliberately at her. The hits had taken their toll.

I won't spend time here detailing Ms. White's personal life—her multiple marriages, affairs, the congressional investigations into her chargeable tax offenses, her salary of $5 million a year and purchase of a $3.5 million condo in Trump Tower, her personal jet, payments of over $1 million per year to her family members—that has been well done and documented by others.

Instead, I will focus on why White now appears on the third level in *Trump's Towering Inferno*, a few floors down from the luxury condo she purchased in 2006.

Paula White

I thought of two biblical passages that Ms. White had either never read or chose to ignore, to her peril:

"He who justifies the wicked is an abomination to the Lord" (NRSV 1991:Proverbs 17: 15).

"Do not store up for yourselves treasures on earth, where moth and rust consume and where thieves break in and steal; but store up for yourselves treasures in Heaven, where neither moth nor rust consumes and where thieves do not break in and steal.

For where your treasure is, there your heart will be also (NRSV 1991:Matthew 6: 19-21).

Not only did White ignore these scriptural texts, but she worked with like-minded individuals to declare Trump's presidency a God-centered theocracy. She claimed, over and over, that Trump was God's chosen man to lead the United States and that to stand against Trump was to stand against God.

Here are but a few of White's comments regarding Trump, with my thoughts in italics:

"When I walk on White House grounds, God walks on White House Grounds. I have every right and authority to declare the White House as Holy Ground because I was standing there and where I stand is holy" (NowThis News, 2019).

This is unbounded nonsense. The White House grounds are not holy ground because she declares they are holy ground. If we are to believe the words of the Bible, it is God who declares Holy Ground, and not any mortal being. Further, every inch of ground on the earth can be understood as Holy Ground: the line between the sacred and profane is thin if it exists at all.

"It is God that raises up a king. It is God that sets one down, and so when you fight against the plan of God you are fighting against the hand of God" (NowThis News, 2019).

Here's the thing: when you say God lifted and chose Trump to be the president (king) of the United States, and that God chooses presidents, don't you imply that God chose Barack Obama to be the previous president?

And every other president? And every other elected official? If God chose Donald Trump to be president of the United States, then, you could argue, God chose Adolf Hitler to be the Führer of Germany.

"To say no to President Trump would be saying no to God, and I won't do that" (NowThis News, 2019).

Does this need a comment? Here is maybe the most obvious reply. The Trump administration had an official policy to separate children at the U.S. border with Mexico. To say "no" to that policy would be to say "yes" to God. This is but one example of many Trump policies that obviously were not Godly.

"Let every demonic network that has aligned itself against the purpose against the calling of President Trump, let it be broken, let it be torn down in the name of Jesus."

"Lord, we ask you to deliver our president from any snare, any setup of the enemy, according to Ephesians 6:12. Any persons [or] entities that are aligned against the president will be exposed and dealt with and overturned by the superior blood of Jesus."

"Whether it's the spirit of Leviathan, a spirit of Jezebel, Abaddon, whether it's the spirit of Belial, we come against the strongmen, especially Jezebel, that which would operate in sorcery and witchcraft, that which would operate in hidden things, veiled things, that which would operate in deception . . . We come against it according to your word" (Lemon, 2019).

The trouble with this is that Trump and his advisors considered every opponent of Trump to be demonic. That just simply was not the case.

"Southern California is looking at banning, well, there's already a law, passed through the governor, that says the Bible is a book of hate speech and to ban the sale of it" (NowThis News, 2019).

This is fake news. WTF?

- **Robert Jeffress.** Just to the right of Ms. White stood Robert Jeffress. He was also bloody and bruised. The former pastor of the First Baptist Church of Dallas, he was also a Fox News contributor and outspoken supporter of Donald Trump.

To be fair, Jeffress took an antiracist stance throughout his entire ministry. This is a rare position for many evangelical Christians.

But he was a staunch opponent of same-sex marriage and the LGBT movement, as well as a critic of non-Christian religions, including Judaism, Islam, Mormonism, and Hinduism, saying their followers reject "the truth of Christ" and "will go to Hell if they do not accept Christ." He once said that Islam is a religion that "promotes pedophilia."

Jeffress has a long history of political involvement, but we will begin with his comment on November 12, 2012, when he said Barack Obama was "paving the way for the future reign of the Antichrist." Although he had said in 2011 that Mitt Romney, a Mormon, was "opposed to Christianity," he supported him during his presidential campaign in 2012.

In the 2016 presidential campaign, Jeffress endorsed and appeared at Donald Trump MAGA rallies. He served on Trump's Evangelical Advisory Board and White House Faith Initiative. Among other things, he said the following:

Speaking on Fox News in 2018 and addressing the alleged affair Trump had with Stormy Daniels, Jeffress said, "Even if it's proven to be true, it doesn't matter" (Fox News, 2019).

In September 2019, he again spoke on Fox News, this time to address the (first) impeachment inquiry of Donald Trump. He said, "I have never seen the Evangelical Christians more angry over any issue than this attempt to illegitimately remove this President from office . . . . If the Democrats are successful in removing the President from office, it will cause a Civil-War like fracture in this nation from which our country will never heal" (First Baptist Dallas, 2019).

- **Kenneth and Gloria Copeland**. Next to Jeffress were Kenneth and Gloria Copeland. It's difficult to understand how and why individuals such as the Copeland ever achieved any level of "success" in the real world. But they did!

Kenneth Max Copeland and his wife, ah, *third* wife, Gloria, established the Kenneth Copeland Ministries. Gloria also served as one of President Trump's evangelical ministers.

The Copelands were prosperity gospel preachers. Copeland wrote that his parishioners would get a hundredfold return on their investment through giving to God.

Kenneth earned great public ridicule and criticism after his 2019 interview with Lisa Guerrero on *Inside Edition*, where he defended his and Gloria's lavish lifestyle. They live in a $6.3 million mansion, purchased with a "parsonage allowance" that is not subject to income taxes. The Copelands are worth a reported $300 million.

The church owns three private jets, including a $20 million jet that, in addition to flying them around the world to speaking events, was also used for trips to their vacation homes, ski resorts, and a private game reserve. The Copelands also own their own airport, the Kenneth Copeland Airport, that is part of their compound in Fort Worth, Texas.

Ken argued that his use of the jets was theologically justifiable. He was asked about another televangelist who also owned private jets and said this about him: "He used to fly airlines, but it got to the point where it was agitating him spiritually. He had become famous, and they were wanting him to pray for them and all that. You can't manage that today. This dope filled world. You get in an airplane you get in a long tube with a bunch of demons. And it's deadly."

He also said that without the jets, he would have to give up 65 percent of his ministries because of the wasted time it would take to get to different locations around the world. It was also pragmatic and financially practical to be able to fly nonstop to different locations without having to stop and refuel.

Gloria Copeland was a preacher herself. In addition to the heretical prosperity gospel message that she and her husband preached, she also said that children do not need the flu shot because Jesus had already "bore our sickness. We don't have a flu season," she continued, "and don't receive it when somebody's threatening you with 'everybody's getting the flu.' We've already had our shot. He bore our sickness and carried our diseases."

I stepped back from the front row and the six individuals I had been speaking with. Sure enough, I was not struck or hurt by any of the stones being thrown. But the stones had been flying, over my head, striking those in the second and third rows from the front. I thought for a moment that I recognized a former colleague, a Southern Baptist pastor who it was said condemned more men and women to Hell than God. Maybe that was true.

A group of stoners (the only other time I had ever heard the word "stoners" used in a sentence was in reference to a cadre of marijuana smokers) approached the middle of the room with large, smooth rocks in their hands. They had been holding back, waiting for me to withdraw. Together they threw the rocks in unison. The men and women in the first row saw the rocks coming but were too slow to avoid them. The rocks did their damage. The punishment had resumed.

It occurred to me that these men and women with whom I had just spoken, like everyone else on this third level of *Trump's Towering Inferno*, were like the men and women I had met through my decades at clergy associations. There were always members of the Christian Right in the towns where I served as a United Methodist pastor. Many were overtly racist. They supported Republican candidates and presidents like Ronald Reagan, W, and Trump. They were anti-Muslim, anti-LGBT, and anti-Semitic. They supported U.S. wars and military spending. They brought the flags of the U.S. military departments into their sanctuaries as if these departments were holy (Army, Navy, Marine Corps, Air Force, Coast Guard, and Space Force). They were against undocumented immigration and downplayed the seriousness of COVID-19.

Following meetings, I would speak to my progressive clergy friends, and we would shake our heads and wonder why we had such different views. I know it is related to worldview and our different understanding of both Christianity and the world, but still, it often seemed as though we were members of different religions. I felt badly for them. At least a little bit.

I mentioned this to the General. He sighed and said, "Judgement is never easy to see. These men and women are heretical charlatans who 1) fleeced their flock enabling them to live extravagant lives of the rich and famous, 2) helped elevate Donald Trump to messianic levels, 3) promoted anti-Christian teaching by spreading anger and hatred, 4) failed to protect their flocks by denying the dangers of COVID-19 to stay fully aligned with President Trump, and finally, 5) hurt the Christian Church by giving it a black eye through their high-profile activities and large personalities.

"For this, they will be stoned. For eternity. In life, anyone can stop, look in the mirror and turn around. Individuals can give back the money they conned from their supporters. They can apologize for their lies. They can stand for peace with justice for all the world's people, including those living in poverty, people of color, and those living in other nations and worshipping God through other religions. They can atone for their unlimited support of Donald Trump. They can do this while walking on the planet. But once they have departed the earth, it is too late. They already abandoned hope long before they got here.

"Time to move forward," he sighed, and so we did. I was happy to be finished with another level, one that struck home to me as a former member of the clergy.

CHAPTER 4

FOURTH FLOOR: GOVERNORS WHO DO MORE HARM THAN GOOD

Three blind mice, three blind mice
They are not very nice, not very nice.
They all went after the cheese at once
They thought it would make an easy lunch.
They lied and they cheated and denied too much.
Three blind mice, three blind mice.

We headed back to the staircase, a modest set of industrial steps. Dust gathered along the edges of each landing; steps are seldom used because most Trump Tower residents take the elevators if they ascend any higher than the second floor, from which they would have used the infamous escalator.

As we climbed the stairs, I asked Arnold about a specific event where our lives overlapped.

"General," I said, "I am curious about your experience and memories from the Battle of Ridgefield. I am . . ."

"Yes, I know." He said, interrupting. "I've done my research on you. I know that you were raised in Ridgefield, Connecticut, scene of the Battle of Ridgefield during the Revolutionary War."

"Cool," I said.

"Do you really think so? It's actually getting hotter as we move higher in *Trump's Towering Inferno*." Apparently, colonials did not say "Cool." I let it go.

"Battle of Ridgefield. April. 27, 1777," he said crisply, his memory sharp and accurate. He looked off into the distance, perhaps hearing the gun and cannon discharges, smelling the gunpowder and seeing the scenes from that fateful day again in his mind.

"You were there. In fact, your deeds were declared heroic by General Washington, the Continental Congress, and military and even political leadership on British side."

Arnold turned toward me but stared past me into the distance.

I continued, "You had a horse shot out from under you, and had your leg trapped under the horse. You refused to concede to a British soldier, saying 'Not yet' when he asked you to surrender. You then were able to free your revolver and fatally shot him. You pulled yourself free, rallied the American troops, slowed down the British and had another horse shot out from you the next day."

He kept staring. "Make your point or ask a question."

"John Adams moved that Congress should strike a medal with your likeness on both sides. He said: 'I wish we could make a beginning, by striking a medal with a platoon firing at General Arnold, on horseback, his horse falling dead under him and he deliberately disentangling his feet from the stirrups and taking his pistols out of his holsters before his retreat.' Then, on the back side, Arnold 'should be mounted on a fresh horse, receiving another discharge of musketry, with a wound in the neck of his horse.' Adams thought your courage was such as the world had rarely witnessed (Martin, 1997: 322). Do you have anything to say about that battle?"

He turned his gaze from me and stared off into the distance again.

"I shot and killed, right in front of me, several British soldiers that day. I commanded all the American soldiers that day, and many more through the years, who were either wounded or killed in battles I led. I killed many other soldiers, most British, but some Americans after I switched sides. It was your General Sherman who spoke it best: 'I confess without shame that I am tired and sick of war. Its glory is all moonshine. Even success, the most brilliant is over dead and mangled bodies . . . . It is only those who have not heard a shot, nor heard the shrills and groans of the wounded and lacerated (friend or foe) that cry aloud for more blood and more vengeance.' And in another speech, Sherman said simply, 'War is Hell.' Sherman was correct. No one should ever brag or glorify or extol their war exploits.

"There's a memorial on Main Street in Ridgefield that stands just off from where the major fighting took place," he continued. Recent excavations, I knew, had turned up skeletons they believe were soldiers from that day's battle. "The memorial says, among other things, these words: 'Died Eight Patriots who were laid in these grounds. Companioned by sixteen British Soldiers. Living, their enemies: Dying their guests.' One of those buried there is the young man who summoned me to surrender. Had I done as he demanded, he would have lived, maybe survived the war, returned to England, started a family. Standing here in *Trump's Towering Inferno*, I know what literal Hell is. But war is as close to Hell on earth as you can experience. And that's all I have to say about the Battle of Ridgefield."

We continued up the stairwell without further comment and arrived at a door with the number "4" on it. I watched as the general reached for and grasped the doorknob, turned it, and opened the door.

What horrors would this floor hold? Who might I meet here? I took a deep breath as the door opened onto the fourth level of *Trump's Towering Inferno*.

Like every other level, the scene that met my eyes confirmed that I was not in Connecticut anymore.

This space in front of me was rather small, on the scale and layout of a normal-sized living room. I saw a sofa and matching love seat, a reclining chair, coffee table, bookshelf, and large-screen TV mounted on a wall. Everything seemed normal except . . . the room was filled with cats, 10 or 12 of them, maybe more. There were striped cats and spotted cats and cats that were all black, or white, or orange. Some were sleeping, some were awake: a few of the cats that were awake stared at the door, while others seemed to be on the hunt, crouched down and creeping slowly across the room. Some were sitting on the sofas and chairs, one was perched high on the bookshelf, while others were sprawled on the floor. Occasionally, one would pounce on something small in front of it. The cats, I realized, were chasing mice.

"Cats and mice," I said to the General.

"You'll see."

I also saw a large chunk of cheese in the middle of the room.

The mice were hiding under the furniture, peeking out from time to time: they were scanning the room for cats. A mouse suddenly darted forward, making a run at the cheese.

As it neared its dairy target, a cat sprang forward and quickly overtook the mouse. It knocked the mouse off its feet with a quick swipe of its paw, then quickly snatched the mouse in its mouth and moved away from the cheese. The mouse struggled to free itself, but the cat simply bit down harder: I heard the mouse squeal in pain.

"Okay, what's going on here?"

"Well, you just watched that cat catch a mouse. The cat will likely 'play' with that mouse for some time before killing and eating it. It will be over for that mouse in the next 30 to 60 minutes. And by the way, the mouse was Kristi Noem, former governor of South Dakota during the Trump presidency," he stated.

"*What*?"

"That mouse was Governor Noem. The mice you see here are what we call the 'Trump Governors,' those who sought political advantages and exploited their people's voting behavior and ignorance by supporting policies and laws that hurt their people. You have always heard that there is a special place in Hell for those who deliberately cause harm to others, especially those for whom they are entrusted to care for. Well, this is that *special* place for Trump's governors.

"There is a special place in Hell for Saddam Hussein, who gassed his own people. There is a special place in Hell for Joseph Stalin, for Adolf Hitler and Pol Pot, for Mao Zedong, for Jim Jones, and many, many more. But this is the place in Hell for the governors who publicly supported Donald Trump so that their political careers might benefit, to the detriment of their constituents."

I couldn't think of anything to say. Arnold grinned at me.

"What's the matter?" he asked playfully. "Cat got your tongue?" He held up a palm. "Just messing with you. These governors were evil leaders. They scored political points by advocating policies that hurt their own people and led to thousands and thousands of deaths in their states and across the nation. Their support of Trump and his lies helped weaken the United States internally and on the global stage. They lied about global climate change. They lied about the efficacy of masks and vaccinations during the COVID-19 crisis. They lied about the dangers of immigration and undocumented individuals living in the United States. They lied about The Big Lie, parroting the line that the 2020 election was stolen from Trump by Biden. This encouraged their people to believe that Biden was not the legitimate president and thus weakened Biden's administration and the office of the president. Further, The Big Lie helped these governors to pass legislation in their states that made it more difficult for people of color to vote, therefore suppressing democracy. They put their own political aspirations above the interests of children's health by decreeing a no-mask mandate in public schools. This is, by *definition*, evil.

"Like Trump and everyone else in this *Towering Inferno*, they were traitors, turncoats, men and women who left their states weaker after they left office than when they started their terms. Like Trump, they lied for personal gain."

"What happened to them?" I asked. "Didn't they believe what they were advocating for?

"No, of course not," he replied. "Their policies and their positions were not based on fact, science, or personal convictions. Their political positions were based purely on strategy and self-interests. Their strategy was simple: divide and conquer. Create an enemy—be it Muslims, Mexicans, blacks, members of the LGBT community, Democrats, liberals, progressives. Feminists, environmentalists. Doctors, scientists, teachers, and professors. Hollywood, the elite, or whomever. Then, go on the attack. The more extreme the charge, the louder they yelled and more they fought. Remember the first lesson taught in public speaking 101, or any oratory class, is that when your argument is weak, you speak louder, and when your argument is complete bollocks, you scream.

"The screaming and yelling from these men and women was offensive and dangerous. They knew that in a divided nation they would not need 50 percent of the people to support them. Consider this: Trump won the presidency in 2016 with only 46.1 percent of the popular vote and almost won again in 2020 with 46.9 percent. Divide and conquer. Use gerrymandering to gain a political advantage in elections. Don't bring the nation together, but rather rally your base behind you. Fire them up with lies. Create false enemies and go after them. Then insist there is rampant voter fraud and pass laws that make it difficult for minorities to vote. You win by getting your base to the polls and suppressing the votes of your opposition. Simple math.

"Trump saw his path to a second term through a strong turnout among his base and support from some moderates if the economy was strong. He saw the pandemic as an existential threat to his re-election campaign because he thought it would hurt the economy, his supposed strong suit. So, he lied about the dangers of COVID-19 publicly while at the same time demonstrating he knew its danger in interviews with Bob Woodrow. He downplayed it right through the election and beyond. He explicitly refused to follow the guidance of national and world medical leaders during the COVID-19 pandemic and even claimed that he knew more about the disease than did the doctors and infectious disease specialists!

"He demeaned, derided, and disparaged professional scientists, medical researchers, and doctors. He denied the science that was being developed to mitigate the effects of COVID-19 so that he could keep the economy strong, thereby giving him a better chance to win re-election.

"As Republican governors during the time of Trump, they did what he did and followed his lead. Call them mini-

Trumps, or Trumps 2.0. They did not implement mask mandates and raised doubt about the efficacy and even the potential dangers of wearing masks. They refused to protect the lives of children in their states. Using and risking the health and safety of children in the public schools for personal political gain under the guise of defending 'liberty' is a cunning form of child sacrifice and is strongly condemned by God and civilized societies.

"They are also strong defenders of the Second Amendment, with near perfect scores from the NRA. Each of them has opposed common-sense gun control legislation that 1) makes sense, 2) receives between 70 and 90 percent support in public opinion polls, and 3) would have saved thousands of lives. The Heavenly hosts are upset with every shooting, even more so with mass shootings, then angrier when we hear from these Republican leaders that 'our thoughts and prayers go out to the victims and their families at this tragic time, and in light of a time for mourning, this is no time for discussing gun control legislation and this is more of a mental health issue and the only thing that can stop a bad guy with a gun is a good guy with a gun and guns have been a part of the United States since its settlement over 400 years ago and blah blah blah blah blah blah.'

"In addition, it has been calculated that three quarters of the deaths in the United States from COVID-19 can be attributed to the polices of the Trump Administration and these governors. They could have taken and enforced more effective policies and did not.

"If Donald Trump, like any other rational leader, had taken the pandemic seriously from the beginning, hundreds of thousands of lives could have been saved. He could have, and should have, encouraged mask wearing, social distancing and online work and learning. He did, it is true, support

'Operation Warp Speed,' but any idiot would have done the same. Once the vaccine was available, he and these governors and other Republican leaders got the vaccines ASAP but were tepid and sometimes even skeptical of their need and effectiveness to their people. They opened the door for the crazy Q-Anon conspiracy claims that led to millions and millions of Americans refusing to get jabbed, thus leading to more death and suffering. They failed to provide leadership during this difficult time.

"They have blood on their hands from their denials of the dangers of COVID-19 and the mass shootings that take place daily in the United States. They are no better than Judas, who betrayed his master for 30 pieces of silver: they exchanged their constituencies for funding and support from the NRA and votes from their unhinged base.

"They knew better. Full stop. They also knew global climate change was real, human driven, and radically changing planet earth. Their denial of this reality was not based in the phony, petroleum-industry-sponsored articles and essays they cited, but in the strategy of getting donations from these same industries and keeping their voters misinformed about the existential threat to the world's population from climate change." The general paused after this rant.

"Okay, so why is there a big block of cheese in the middle of the room? Are the mice starving and trying to get some food?"

"No, not really. The cheese is there as food that mice like, true. But this is more symbolic. The Big Cheese is Donald Trump himself. These mini-Trump governors are attracted to the cheese like children to chocolate. It is the bait the cats use to entice the mice out from their hiding spaces, so they can catch them."

Just then, another mouse made a run for the cheese, its tiny legs running at full speed to reach it. But, as the mouse sprinted toward the cheese, two cats sprang simultaneously at it. They headed it off just before the mouse was able to reach the cheese. They batted it back and forth between them, with savage blows from their paws, claws extended. The mouse, badly wounded, ended up in the mouth of a striped cat, who carried it back to a corner where I could hear it crunching down on its bones and consuming it in pieces.

"Who was that?"

"That was Greg Abbott, of Texas."

I stood silent for a moment, trying to absorb what I had just seen.

"There is Ron DeSantis over in the corner," Arnold said. "Would you like to speak to him before he makes a run for the cheese?"

"OK," I stuttered. Other than a one-way conversation I had as a child with Mickey Mouse on the television as a child, I had never spoken to a mouse before.

"Don't think of him as a mouse," Arnold stated. "But as the former governor of Florida and failed presidential candidate as the nominee of the Republican Party."

I walked unsteadily toward the small mouse hiding under the reclining chair and stooped over. "Governor DeSantis?" I asked.

"Yes?" he squeaked.

"Can I ask you a few questions?"

"Yes but make it quick." His beady eyes darted to the cheese in the center of the room. "I am looking to make a run for

Ron DeSantis

president again and need the support of the Great One, the Big Cheese, the man who made America Great before the Deep State, libs and fake news media made his re-election impossible in 2020."

"You know that didn't happen," I said.

His little beady eyes looked at me as if seeing me for the first time.

"Oh, I thought you were one of my supporters. Yes, of course

75

I know he didn't win the 2020 election. We all knew that. I just kept saying that because that's what he believed and what his base wanted. See, I needed his support. I needed his base. I have carefully studied the way he won the presidency. His instincts were brilliant. Lie, deceive, distract, distort. Create enemies and attack them. Divide and conquer. His strategy worked for him and will work for me."

"But there is a better way, a higher way, yes," I stated. "I mean, you are a graduate of Yale University. You attended Harvard Law School and were a Naval JAG officer with service in Iraq. You had the world at your command. But you chose the path of lies and deception!"

"I chose the path to triumph and success," he insisted. "I thought about this often. Although Florida was teetering on becoming a purple state, it was still red. That means the state still leaned Republican. It meant they believed in and followed Donald Trump. It meant they accepted his lies. This was all part of my plan of how I won election to Congress, the governor's mansion and, my grand prize, how I would win the White House."

"But you exposed the children of Florida to harm by banning mask mandates. You opposed the Patient Protection and Affordable Care Act. You banned the teaching of critical race theory in Florida even though it has never been part of the curriculum. You opposed gun regulations and received an A+ rating from the NRA. You supported an 'antimob' extension to the stand-your-ground law in Florida that would allow gun-owning citizens to use deadly force on individuals they thought might be looting."

"These policies were popular among the Trump base, so, yes, I supported them," he said.

"And you regret none of these decisions?"

"In hindsight, maybe, because it turns out that while this strategy worked for Trump in 2016, lying your way to the top is not a good way to stay at the top. There are just too many good people in the United States. There are too many solid journalists and writers who did a better job of calling my lies out. Too many of Trump's base of older, white voters died of COVID-19, leaving me high and dry with a younger, more-mixed-race voting bloc. The Q-Anon conspiracies couldn't be credibly sustained because too many of their wild predictions didn't come to pass. I made a mistake using this strategy because it was not successful: I don't regret having a strategy of lying and deception, though, because I thought it would work.

"Americans hate being told what to do! Exploiting divisive issues stoked outrage. It's such a great political tool to make Americans feel their freedom is under attack. It was great and almost worked!"

"Don't you care those hundreds of thousands of American lives could have been saved by wearing masks? We could have united the country around safety?" I was angry at this point.

"Politics is about getting votes and going on the attack in anger gets votes! Honest to God, you liberals are such naifs! Voters were angry about lockdowns, about mask mandates, about having their guns taken away and wanting to live their lives as they chose and not pandering to the New Green Deal, supported by tree-hugging environmentalists. We almost won! We came so close. It would have been much harder to create a movement to unite folks by mask mandates and caring for others. Where is the political fire there? I fail to see the point."

"The point is saving lives and doing the right things," I snapped. "The point in public service is serving the public. You used the public. You allowed your people to die."

"People die every day under every governor and every President," he snapped. "The point of politics is winning, my friend. Politics is a dirty, zero-sum game. You think any politician is different? Stop living in a fantasy dreamland. This world is a struggle of power, and conflict with negative campaigning brings votes, look at the demographics and results."

"Your state is now going underwater due to climate change. You denied science, and the whole planet is now transforming right before our eyes." I was trying my best to 1) remain calm and 2) force him to see the immorality of his methods. Yes, I know, you can't reason with the unreasonable. Why do we keep trying? I can't explain it.

"Where are the votes in telling people to cut down consumption?" DeSantis countered. "Slow down the economy? Talk about global climate change? Please stop. How would I get people out to the polls by saying that the world is dying around them? Climate change is a boring political issue, hopeless, with no clear solution. You think any politician would solve it? All politicians are the same, my friend. What would be the point in bringing that up, how would it help me politically to tell this 'inconvenient truth?'"

"But people suffered, their homes were destroyed. Half our country was on fire and half flooded. The beautiful coral reefs and coastlines of your state, gone. Isn't this worth more than politics to save the earth?"

"You are such a chump. Politics is a dirty game of money and power. I needed the oil and donations to flow, the highways full. The earth is going down the drain anyway. We needed donations! How exactly would I win elections talking about these sad things you speak of?" He broke off our conversation. "Excuse me for a second—the cats are distracted, and I need a piece of that cheese."

He sprinted toward the cheese. It was like watching an accident unfold right before my eyes. I could not turn away, even though I did not want to watch.

The cats were ready. This time, four cats emerged from different parts of the room to chase their prey. One leaped off the coffee table and got to Ron first. She smacked him hard with her paw, sending him tumbling toward the base of the coffee table, where he was slammed to a stop hitting the table leg. She followed up, tossing him into the air, and another cat caught him in her mouth. The four cats hustled to a corner of the room where they began what seemed to be a deliberate torture of the former governor.

"Why cats?" I asked.

"Well, these are barn cats, who have been trained at catching mice and vermin for thousands of years. These governors had the ability to improve the lives of their people. They had that direction toward which they could have pushed. Instead, they chose the easier, lesser path. They are fated to experience this recurring reality: each day, they wake up, alive again, determined to get to the Big Cheese, only to be caught, tortured by the cats, and, eventually, killed and eaten.

"The governors were unpleasant rodents. They are represented by mice. The cats, like the Capitol Hill police officers, are the enforcers of the penalties imposed on these governors. They will chase these vermin for eternity."

"So, this is like Groundhog *Day*? Are Bill Murray and Andie MacDowell nearby?"

He stared at me for a moment with that penetrating and harsh look: "This is reality, Dr. Lavender, not Hollywood. They awaken each day and end each day tends he same way. This will go on for eternity. This is Hell.

"To be sure, politicians have always bent the truth. There have been lies told since the founding of this great nation. But honesty has always been the ideal, the goal, and the expectation for elected officials in the United States. Let's remember that when young Abraham Lincoln made a mistake, overcharging one of his customers $0.065 (6 and ½ cents, yes, we used to have a .5 cent coin). In the middle of the night, he walked three miles after the store closed to return the woman's money. Another time, he mistakenly gave a customer a quarter pound of tea because the scale had been set at that weight earlier, instead of the half pound of tea that had been ordered and paid for. Lincoln walked well into the night to give the man the remainder of the tea.

"Donald Trump and his cronies, including these governors, brought lying to a whole new level. Their lies contributed to the deaths of Americans, so they are properly placed here. Other governors here include Tate Reeves, Kevin Stitt, Mike Parsons, Bill Lee, and Doug Ducey."

We'd seen what there was to see; our time on this level was coming to an end. I stepped across the room for a final look. I glanced at the large screen television. I had not noticed what it was showing until just now. Here was *The Cat in the Hat*, the American animated musical television special that first aired in 1971 on CBS that was based on Dr. Seuss's children's book of the same name.

"They get to watch *The Cat in the Hat*," I noted.

"It's on the telly, yes," the General replied. "But I'm not sure they actually watch it. It's more of a metaphor for everyone involved here, the governors, the cats, observers. Early in 2021, the Dr. Seuss Enterprises (DSE) decided, after the recommendation of a panel they formed, to stop publishing six of the books they hold the copyrights to because of their racist and insensitive imagery. This decision was made by the DSE, which includes members of the family of Theodor Seuss Geisel (Dr. Seuss) and other supporters of this popular writer.

"Republican leaders, including some of these governors, used that decision to go on the offensive, as usual. They blamed the Democrats and the Progressives, the press, the libs, and the politically correct police around the nation. There is no bar too low for them to go under. You see, the decision to stop publishing these books was made by the family and supporters of Geisel's work, and not by the 'woke liberals.' Here on the fourth level of *Trump's Towering Inferno,* where the governors lose an existential game of life and death with these barn cats every day, *The Cat in the Hat* is a playful reminder that telling the truth should always be the rule."

We returned to the staircase and made our exit from this feline floor.

CHAPTER 5

FIFTH FLOOR: PROFESSIONAL LIARS

> Roses are red
> Violets are blue
> Trump is a pathological liar
> His press secretaries were too.

We climbed the stairs in silence. I had a lot to think about, and the general seemed to understand. On the fifth-floor landing, Arnold turned and asked, "All right? Ready to move on?"

I shrugged and pulled in a deep breath. "Let's keep going, I think."

"It's not going to get any easier," Arnold said, "but I think it best to move forward. Otherwise, you will just worry about what is to come. My approach was always to press ahead, and I think you are a like-minded person."

I nodded. Maybe I was that.

Arnold turned the doorknob and we walked through the door to level five of *Trump's Towering Inferno*.

We stepped into a hospital room. Its bright lights contrasted with the dusky previous levels and murky stairwell. We paused for a few minutes so our eyes could adjust to the new conditions, and to take in the scene unfolding before us.

Doctors and nurses moved around the room, carrying charts, needles, and other medical equipment. I saw what appeared to be three stations, in three separate locations, for treatment. Three individuals, two women and a man, were being treated, one at each station. After receiving their treatment, a bell rang, and the three moved forward to the next location.

As we walked further into the room, I recognized the three individuals. They were Sean Spicer, Sarah Sanders, and Kayleigh McEnany, press secretaries during the presidency of Donald Trump.

"Trump had four press secretaries during his administration," Arnold said. "These three, Spicer, Sanders, and McEnany, and a fourth, Stephanie Grisham. Grisham was Trump's third press secretary. She served for over a year and held that position between the times of Sanders and McEnany. She is the only presidential press secretary in history who never held a press conference. She made appearances on Fox and other conservative news outlets but refused to meet the White House press corps for a regular press conference. Grisham was another Trump supporter who had no problem blurring the lines between truth and lies, and she made some crazy statements about Trump, including defending his 'genius.' But the Heavenly panel determining her eternal fate was divided on her placement, so she is still in limbo, awaiting a final decision.

"What you see here are Trump's best-known press secretaries. These three individuals received, in salaries and benefits, more than $200,000 per year for their work. So, we like to say it is not about the money. But they were paid and paid well. They were paid to lie. They supported the Great Liar and Traitor. They were paid liars, professional perjurers, porkies, individuals who spun, lied, distracted, deflected, and defended the indefensible Donald Trump."

We walked forward. As we approached the stations, a bell went off, and the three press secretaries were led by a hospital administrator from one treatment center to the next around a small, central island.

We came to our first station, where Sean Spicer was receiving his "treatment." Sean served as Trump's first press secretary and held that office for less than six months, beginning on January 20, 2017. During that time, he deliberately lied to the press corps and to the American public. His first big whopper came on his second day of work, January 21, 2017, the day after Trump's inauguration, when he claimed that the crowd at that event was the "largest audience to ever to witness an inauguration, period—both in person and around the globe." He defended this statement in the following days, using doctored statistics from the Washington D.C., Metro, and from the official police estimates of the crowd. These lies were patently false, as anyone could see from the photos and actual numbers released from the Metro and police department, but Sean dug in deeper on this petty, but foretelling, subject. If you are willing to lie about crowd sizes when everyone can see you are lying, you are willing to lie about anything.

This "first lie" brought senior presidential advisor Kelly Anne Conway (we'll see her higher in the tower) into the conversation. Her infamous phrase, "alternative facts," was ginned up in reference to Sean Spicer's and the administration's claim that this was the largest crowd ever to attend an inauguration. In defending the bald-faced lie, she stated, in essence, that facts don't matter and can be manipulated and used for the ends they pursued.

Spicer, channeling Trump, wanted the American public to believe that Trump's presidency was off to a great start and that the new president had tremendous public support and adulation. The facts show that Trump received almost three million fewer votes than Hillary Clinton in that same election, and the turnout for his inauguration was well below the crowds Barack Obama and Bill Clinton drew, and similar to the crowd George W. Bush had at his inaugurations.

What struck many American citizens, and others around the world, was that, if Spicer and other spokespersons for Donald Trump were willing to lie about this nonpolicy issue, what would they do with issues that really mattered? If there are alternative facts, where does the truth live? Does the truth even matter anymore? Sean set the tone for the Trump administration: this was going to be a presidency where facts simply did not matter; no matter how petty the issue or policy, lies, misinformation, and disinformation would be the order of the day.

Sean arrived at a sterile nursing station. There were several nurses and a doctor at hand. The nurses told Sean to open his mouth. He refused. The nurses sprang into action and forced his mouth to open by leveraging his jaws apart. Once Spicer's mouth opened a crack, they shoved in a small device with a lever. Pumping it, they opened his oral cavity as wide as if for a dentist.

Once his mouth was opened, the nurses converged with bars of lava soap and sponges. They scrubbed Spicer's mouth, in and out, with the soap, then brought over a garden hose. At a command, a faucet was turned, and water began streaming out of the hose, which was positioned directly in front of Sean's mouth. He coughed and wheezed like a drowning man. While technically, this would not be described as waterboarding, I think the results were about the same. Spicer was gagging, shaking, crying, and pleading.

A couple of steps to the right took us to the station where Sarah Sanders was receiving her treatment. Having just come from the extreme mouth washing and rinsing location herself, Sarah's clothing was dripping, and she looked exhausted as she struggled to catch her breathe.

Nurses flanked her on each side. A third raised and tested a syringe that would be used to inject her. Sarah struggled, but the guardian nurses only held her more securely. The nurse with the syringe inserted the needle into Sarah's arm, shoved the plunger home, then pulled the device away and discarded it. The medication nurse filled an empty glass with clear fluid from a beaker. She proffered the glass to Sarah, who refused it. Once again, the guardians at either elbow stepped in, forcing Sarah's mouth open and pouring the fluid down her throat. Sanders swallowed and made a pained and angry face.

"What is happening here?" I asked.

"This is the disinfectant station. Each of these liars, after their mouths are washed and rinsed, gets an injection of bleach and a glass of Lysol. You'll remember that Trump mused out load that that injecting and drinking disinfectants might cure COVID-19 in infected patients."

"But injecting bleach and drinking Lysol can kill people." I stated the obvious.

"Yes, exactly," replied the general. "And that's exactly what Trump did. He killed people with "alternative facts." Did the persons located nearest the truth—these press flacks—ever take exception? Raise questions? Correct misperceptions? They did nothing of the kind but supported him and enabled this behavior to continue unchallenged for four years."

Sarah's arm swelled angrily where the injection was administered. Wincing, she glanced at it and gently touched the area with a forefinger. Suddenly she grabbed her stomach and vomited loudly past her lap and onto the gurney. I didn't recall the yellow detergent having red flecks when she drank it, so assumed she must be bringing up blood with the disinfectant. The nurses watched her with neither curiosity nor compassion. I think the General and I had seen as much as we needed to, also, as he pulled my elbow to guide me toward the third and final station.

Here Kayleigh McEnany, still in pain from the mouth washing and rinse, as well as struggling with the toxic doses of bleach and Lysol, was again flanked by two nurses. A third approached with an exposed light bulb attached to a brown electric cord.

The nurse with the bulb commanded, "Open up."

Kayleigh shook her head defiantly. The nurse gave her an icy smile. "Honey, you know you can't resist. This will be over a lot sooner if you cooperate."

"Liar," Kayleigh spat. "I'll fight back as long as I possibly can."

The cold smile got toothier. "That's your choice, I guess." She nodded to the flanking guardians, who pinned Kayleigh's arms expertly, pried her jaws open, and shoved the light bulb down her throat. I wish I could have written "dropped," but the truth is that there was a good deal of shoving and gagging involved. Muffled screams came from somewhere deep inside the scrum of people around the former press secretary. When the let her sit up, tears streamed down her face while lazy drool rolled down the cord that trailed from her mouth all the way to the floor.

After a few moments, the nurses pulled the light bulb out. Kayleigh rolled on the floor clutching her chin and fluttering a hand from her throat to her gut. The nurses let her writhe for a moment, then with outstretched arms helped her back to her feet so she could start the rotation through the punishment stations all over again.

The General nudged me. "Remember when Trump said getting light into the body might kill COVID-19? Like all we had to do to end the pandemic was swallow a bunch of flashlights. Anyway, this is the Dr. Trump Practicing-Medicine-Without-A-License level in Hell, as played out for these three reprobates." A bell rang, each of the three moved forward a station, doomed to migrate from soap and water to disinfectants to electric lighting and back again for all eternity.

"I don't envy them."

"You shouldn't," said the General. "As you saw, they experience three kinds of punishment, one right after the other. You should be here on Tuesdays, when instead of the throat, the burning light bulb is inserted somewhere else. Trump did not say how or where the light should be inserted, but there are only a few options. These are the punishments for the press secretaries who supported and enabled the president, and who lied themselves in their official capacity to the people of the United States.

"Now, we noted earlier previous presidents have lied to the American public. For example, FDR lied about U.S. support to Britain between 1939 and 1941 and concealed the extent of the Pearl Harbor damage and the Navy's early lack of success in the Pacific. We know that Lyndon Baines Johnson lied to the American public about the war in Vietnam. Richard Nixon lied about Watergate and Vietnam. George W. Bush, encouraged by Cheney, lied about Iraq, its relationship to Bin Laden and its nuclear capacity."

"Trump, though, took lying to an entirely new level. As noted earlier, Trump told a staggering 30,573 lies during his four years in office, an average of 21 per day (Kessler, Rizzo, and Kelly, 2021). Trump called the press 'truly the enemy of the people'(March 2019), the same phrase used by Joseph Stalin. I know that dealing with the press corps in an open and free society has never been easy, but this brazen refusal to approach the truth in this administration has empowered other politicians to be just as rude and defiant, and justice must be meted out."

"Should I speak with them?" I asked.

"If you wish. You won't persuade them to change any of their stories, but maybe you'll learn something. Step this way."

Arnold led me through a side door. We walked down a short hallway, then turned to our left. We were in another hallway, with a door up ahead on the left. A few steps took us there. Arnold opened the door and led me into the room behind it.

Somehow, some way, we were in the James S. Brady Press Briefing Room, a small theater located in the West Wing of the White House where official press briefings are given to the news media by the White House press secretaries. Occasionally, the president addresses the press and the nation from this same podium.

Arnold and I moved toward the front row of seats in a room otherwise empty. He encouraged me to have a seat in the first row, right in front of the podium. I turned to the general, who took a seat next to me. "I thought I was going to get to ask some questions?"

"You will be given a short, private briefing, by these three press secretaries. After their opening statements, you will be allowed to ask a few questions."

Spicer was led into the room. He was dressed in a dark suit and tie and looked a bit edgy. He proceeded to deliver the same message he gave at his first official press conference, where he dressed down the media and established "an us-against-them scenario." I share these notes of his short announcement:

- Sean called out a reporter for irresponsible and reckless reporting because that reporter mistakenly tweeted that a bust of Martin Luther King, Jr, had been removed from the Oval Office. The bust had not been removed, and even though the reporter had retracted and apologized for the tweet, Sean called it irresponsible reporting and offensive to the president.

- He then accused the media of "intentionally framing" the inauguration crowd to look smaller than it was, thus hurting the new president. Spicer further said that the ground covers placed on the mall made the crowd look smaller than it was, and that these ground coverings had never been used before (though they had been used before).

- Sean stated that no one could estimate crowd size, including estimating how many were at that day's Woman's March on Washington anti-Trump protest.

- He then said that Trump had drawn the "largest audience to witness an inauguration period, both in person and around the world." He did not provide any means in which to support this claim, nor did this statement line up with the previous statement about there being no way to count how many were at such events.

- Spicer praised the president's speech at the CIA that day, telling the assembled press "That's what you guys should be covering."

- He then warned the journalists, telling them "I'm gonna tell you that it goes two ways. We're gonna hold the press accountable as well" (Lind 2017).

Arnold turned to me. "You have just witnessed, in person, Spicer's first press conference. Although the press secretary took no questions that day, in honor of your visit, you have an opportunity to go back in time and ask a few questions. So go ahead and ask."

I nodded. "Mr. Spicer," I began, "It is empirically verifiable that the crowd for Trump's inauguration was small. Expert crowd-size estimators suggest that the attendance at Trump's inauguration was about twenty-five percent of what Obama drew in 2009, and under half of what Obama drew in 2013. Bill Clinton drew about twice as many people as Trump when he was inaugurated in 1993, and Trump's crowd size was about that of George W. Bush's two inaugural crowds of 300,000–400,000 people in 2001 and 2005, respectfully. So how can you say Trump's crowd was the 'largest audience to witness an inauguration period, both in person and around the world?'"

Spice jumped at the bait. "We maintain that it was the largest crowd ever for an inauguration in U.S. history. We have Washington, D.C., Metro statistics, police estimates, and aerial photos to support that evidence."

"Except none of those things support your story."

"What do *you* know? The crowd size only looks small because of the lawn coverings placed on the D.C. mall. The data released by the Metro were skewed low to make Trump look bad. It is part of the Deep State conspiracy to make President Trump seem weak. Same with the police data. It was the largest crowd ever. It was huge."

"Sean," I asked, "what's the point of this? Why are you lying to us?"

"I am not lying. It is part of my job to project strength and confidence in the presidency. Lies are in the eye of the beholder," Spice stated. "What I am doing is defending and serving as a promoter of the 45th president of the United States. President Trump is tired of people reminding him that he lost the general election to Hillary Clinton by over two and a half million votes. He is sick of people calling him a racist and misogynist. He is eager to 'Make America Great Again,' and can't do it unless we prove to the American public that Trump won legitimately and had great support from the people. It is impossible, and unseemly, to think that Bill Clinton had larger crowds, not to mention the idea that Barack Obama drew more people to his inaugurations than President Trump. We need to project strength, numbers, and overwhelming support."

"So, you are denying that Obama and Clinton had higher crowd totals."

Spicer shook his head. "Of course not. Not really. They had higher crowd totals. Look, don't quote me on this, but we all knew what we were doing. Kelly Anne, myself, his children, the cabinet members. We were not stupid. But Trump gave us his marching orders, his commands. I had to say those things, or the president would be angry and likely fire me."

"So, you lied?"

"I did what needed to be done. I am proud of my time in the administration. Viva la Trump!"

A nurse arrived and took Spicer away. Another arrived, escorting Sarah Sanders, who appeared at the podium in a dark dress.

"You will now be seeing Sarah Sanders at several press conferences. She will be, as usual, contentious, combative, and antagonistic toward the press. Her prickly behavior is exactly what Trump liked about her: she mirrored his own style with the press and everyone else. She was cut from the same cloth. Her misrepresentations flowed as smoothly and freely as Trump's.

The General said, "This time, you are going to see a compilation of Sanders' moments as press secretary, and just before she was promoted to that position when she filled in for Spicer a few times before officially becoming the press secretary in July 2017."

I watched a motionless Sanders anxiously for a moment, but suddenly she came to life, and began working the room, moving seamlessly from topic to topic and effortlessly refusing to acknowledge news hounds who had offended her or her boss.

Her first statement concerned the firing of James Comey by the president, and she defended that decision by stating that she "heard from countless members of the FBI that are grateful and thankful." Of course, the reality was that the White House received many emails from regional field offices and high-ranking FBI officials who were angry and flabbergasted at Comey's firing.

I watched as she twitched and moved into another moment, still focused on the Comey firing, after Comey accused the president of lying. Sanders said, "I can definitively say the president is not a liar, and I think it's frankly insulting that question would be asked."

She twitched again and now was saying that President Trump "certainly did not dictate a statement released by Donald Trump, Jr. about the 2016 meeting in Trump Tower with the Russians." Never mind that in 2018, President Trump's lawyers acknowledged that the president had dictated said statement.

Another twitch, and she was saying, in reference to payments to porn star Stormy Davis, that "there was no knowledge of any payments from the president" to Daniels. Less than a year later, Rudy Giuliani confirmed that Trump had repaid his lawyer Michael Cohen $130,000 for what Cohen had paid Daniels.

Now, another twitch as she spoke on the family separation policy of the Trump administration, the one that resulted in the separation of parents from their children at the Mexican-U.S. border and the resulting placement of children in cages. Sanders first falsely blamed the Democrats for this policy and then stated that this policy "is very biblical," also patently false.

Another scene, still from 2018, when Sarah refused to say that the media were not the enemy of the people, despite numerous questions and opportunities.

Then, we see her on the Christian Broadcasting Network saying, "God calls all of us to fill different roles at different times, and I think that He wanted Donald Trump to become president."

She froze in place. Arnold nudged me in the ribs and whispered in my ear, "Now, go ahead, ask a few questions."

I remember thinking I needed more time. Where would I

begin with such a staunch defender of our worst president's worst behavior? What would I ask?

The general, seeing me hesitate, suggested, "Why don't you ask about the child separation policy of the Trump administration? That's a good place to begin."

I nodded, dug in, and said, "Ms. Sanders, could you speak to me for a few minutes about the Trump policy of separating children at the U.S. border from their parents, and placing the children in cages?"

She glared at me with that look we grew accustomed to seeing during her term as press secretary. "Well, first, let us be clear that this was a Democratic policy. It was started by President Obama. All we did was maintain it.

"We see immigration as a danger to the people of the United States. Criminals were coming across our borders. Rapist. Drug dealers. Terrorists. Murderers. The Democrats want an open border policy. We want to stop illegal immigration and only accept immigrants who will make American great again. Mexico was sending its worst, and more bad people were flooding into the nation from other Central and Southern American nations. We needed to stop this flood of criminals and gang members.

"We established a firm policy: if you tried to get into the United States with children, we would separate those children from you and send you back where you came from. The children had to be processed. We weren't going to put them in the Ritz, you know, or some other exclusive hotel. So, we did what we did. What you and the fake media might call 'cages' were just holding rooms. They were temporary, and everyone knew it.

"This policy deterred millions of persons from even thinking about coming to America. The moms and dads from shithole countries had to think twice about trying to cross our border because they knew if we caught them, they could lose their children."

"And this was a Democratic policy?" I prompted skeptically.

"Yes. It was the Democrats and Obama's policy. But it was the genius of Donald Trump that made the policy work. So, if you think about it, this was really a Trump policy. A Trump victory. Obama and the Democrats favored an open border. They allowed MS-13 gangs and terrorists in. We built the greatest wall, and we separated the children of criminals from their parents. This was what we did to protect Americans and 'Make America Great' again."

There was no point continuing a conversation with someone constitutionally unable to tell the truth "Enough," I said.

"Yes," he agreed and nodded to Sarah's nurse. On cue, the nurse led Sarah out of the room. In came Kayleigh, flanked by another nurse, who parked her by the podium.

"You will now have the opportunity to see and participate in Kayleigh's first press conference. The date is May 1, 2020."

Kayleigh came to life. She smiled and looked around the room. "I will never lie to you. You have my word on that." The words came out of Kayleigh's mouth smoothly and without hesitation. Dressed in a dark suit coat with a dark top and near perfect makeup, she wore a light-colored cross and necklace (silver?) that stood out sharply against the black background.

"The Trump administration earned many low marks and indeed had even lower moments. You have just seen one

Kayleigh McEnany

of them," the general said. "Following that statement to the press, the people of the United States and people of the world, Ms. McEnany lied. She lied that day. She lied the next day. She lied every day she spoke to the American people. She lied after leaving the White House. Too much yakking and rubbish. I don't think we need to see more of her historic lows. Go ahead and ask her some questions. Are you ready?"

I was. This time, I was ready.

"Ms. McEnany," I began. "Can you comment on that promise you made to the American people during your first press conference, when you said you would never lie? It seems like that statement was itself a lie."

"I promised never to lie to the American public, and I did not, have not, and will not moving into the future," she replied. "As a woman of faith, as a mother of baby Blake, as a person who meticulously prepared at some of the world's hardest institutions, I never lied. I sourced my information. But that will never stop the press from calling me a liar."

I turned toward the general. "Is there any point?" I asked.

"No, of course not. She will stand here lying to you until the end of time. These people are convicted liars because they are born liars. We want to keep moving onward. I think we can go."

A nurse came in and led Kayleigh away as we stood and moved toward the door at the back of the room. We exited the room, turned right, took a few steps, turned right again, and traveled down the short hallway leading back to the hospital room. The three press secretaries had returned to their stations and were moving toward their next "treatments." Kayleigh was about to have her mouth washed out and flushed, Sean was at the injection and ingestion station, and Sarah headed for the light bulb. All seemed in order.

We headed to the stairwell, but as we approached it, Arnold turned and said, "Let's take a break. It's been a long adventure so far." Instead of taking the stairs, we walked past them, down a short corridor, and came to what looked like an elevator. Its doors opened automatically, and we stepped inside. The doors closed. Frankly, I don't know if we went up or down, left, or right, backwards or forward, but after about 30 seconds, the doors opened again. Before us was an unexpected view.

Following Arnold, I walked off the elevator into a familiar scene. It was a Mozambiquan village, or, at the least, the re-creation of a Mozambiquan village. The general had brought me to a comfortable location. He knew that in my work with orphans and vulnerable children, I had made multiple trips to that sub-Saharan African nation since my first trip in 1998. It was in Mozambique where I worked closely with church leaders and pastors to help orphans and vulnerable children. Dozens of the clergy and church members I had befriended through decades of work were present, along with hundreds of orphans. The children looked great—they were well-fed, in new clothing, and happy. There were tables of local food—rice, rolls, vegetables, and fruit. There was singing and dancing—a celebration of life. I was warmly embraced, physically, emotionally, and spiritually. I was among my people, my tribe, and could not have been happier or more at peace.

I thought for a moment. This is the biblical vision of God's peaceful kingdom as described in Isaiah 11:1–9. "No," Arnold said, again reading my thoughts. "This is paradise. You are getting an opportunity to see what paradise looks like."

"Paradise is, in essence, what you create in life and an extension of life. Paul said it well: 'And, in the end, the love you take is equal to the love you make.'"

It took me a moment to realize he was quoting Paul McCartney, not the Apostle Paul.

"Donald Trump was devoid of love. He was filled with anger and animosity. He had no friends. His behavior was repulsive. The truest statement in the Bible is this one: 'Do not be deceived; God is not mocked, for you reap whatever you sow' (NRSV, 1991; Galatians 6:7). Trump sowed hatred: he ended up in Hell. His closest aides and members of his administration, they followed suit. They are here as well."

"Here in Mozambique, though, you get a fresh glimpse of what is possible. You are seeing a place filled with grace, peace, mercy, and love. This *is* the peaceable kingdom—and this *is* what the Apostle Paul spoke of when he wrote to the church he established in Corinth:

> Love is patient; love is kind; love is not envious or boastful or arrogant or rude. It does not insist on its own way; it is not irritable or resentful; it does not rejoice in wrongdoing, but rejoices in the truth. It bears all things, believes all things, hopes all things, endures all things. Love never ends . . . . And now faith, hope, and love abide, these three; and the greatest of these is love. (I Corinthians 13: 4 - 8, 13 NRSV 1991)

Arnold continued, "Let's spend an hour here. Then back to the Tower."

It seemed about right, but that hour passed in a few moments, and it was time to go. Strengthened by food, drink, and sub-Saharan fellowship, we returned to the United States, back to New York City, back to *Trump's Towering Inferno*. I would have preferred to stay in that village.

CHAPTER 6

REPREHENSIBLE REPRESENTATIVES

Trump's supporters stormed the hill
To say that he was president still
They led a violent insurrection
To overturn a just election

Congress chose the right direction
The country made the correct selection
Trump failed the people's inspection
Democracy was saved from infection

The magical time-space elevator returned us to the sixth floor of *Trump's Towering Inferno*. We walked into a room filled with bright lights, loud noises, and crowds of young people. It took just a moment to realize we were in an arcade. I smiled—finally, a place to have fun. Then I caught myself. This is *Trump's Towering Inferno*, a place of torment. Why would there be an arcade in here?

"It's not that kind of arcade," Arnold whispered to me, as usual seeming to read my thoughts. The smile left my face. Of course, this wouldn't be just an arcade.

That said, there were some definite arcade features to this one, including crowds. All around, young men and woman moved from game to game. They were high school and college students, and they seemed delighted to discover that the games were free. I saw skeet ball, video games, whack-a-mole, air hockey, and a shooting gallery. There was a snack bar at one end serving free refreshments.

I asked the General, "Who are these young men and women?"

"They are like the Capitol police officers we met on the first floor, and the nurses we met administering 'treatment' to the press secretaries just below us. They are not real people. Again, think of them as avatars, or physical embodiments of real men and women. They have the physical characteristics of specific individuals, but they are not those persons at all. They represent people but are not people. Does any of that help?"

I shrugged. "I guess. This is a confusing place, for sure. What people do these youngsters represent?" I asked.

"Well, as I said on the first floor, the Capitol Hill police officer avatars represent those officers who were most affected by the insurrection at the U.S. Capitol on January 6, 2021. The nurses and doctors we saw on the previous level represent the nurses and doctors who died of COVID-19 in the line of duty. Maybe you remember back to the years 2020, 2021, and 2022, at the height of the pandemic: many put up yard signs and newspaper ads thanking and expressing appreciation for those in the health care field who were risking their lives to help those who were sick. Many of these health care officials died. But some, most of whom were Trump supporters, verbally and, in some instances, physically attacked these same health care leaders because they were speaking out about the pandemic and warning Americans to take the virus seriously.

"It's not like we couldn't have staffed this level with the avatars of young people who died from COVID, but we chose a different population. The young people you see here are the avatars of high school and college students who were killed in senseless gun violence. Some were victims of mass shootings. Others were killed alone in shoot-outs, drive-bys, accidents and collateral damage.

"The real persons these physical incarnations represent are not here. They are in paradise. They are doing what they want to be doing. They are sailing on the high seas, skiing high in the Sierras, tooling around on motorcycles, hiking in the Appalachians, attending music festivals, surfing off the coast of the Pacific, or mountain biking in Utah. They are doing what they want to be doing and what was denied them by the gunmen who took their lives and by the lax laws that allowed so many killers to obtain their weapons easily and legally."

That understood, I took a closer look at others in the room.

I couldn't help noticing that not everyone in the room was having fun. The heads popping up in whack-a-mole holes weren't "moles," but human heads. The faces being shot at in the shooting gallery weren't cartoon characters or caricatures of bad guys, but real people. The puck on the air hockey table had a face on it as well, and as I walked past the table, I saw that the puck's face was screwed up in pain. Was this an arcade, or some medieval torture chamber?

"Let's mosey down the midway," the General suggested.

We moved deeper into the arcade. Directly in front of us were four "whack a mole" games. Three young women and a young man stood focused on their game stations, with clubs ready. As expected, heads popped up, randomly. The young men and women, prepared, took careful aim and proceeded to unload on their targets. Like the conventional game, heads were popping up and down. But unlike the conventional game, this one had the heads 1) staying up longer, allowing the students ample time to hammer the heads with almost every blow, 2) the heads belonged to real people, 3) the clubs being used to whack the heads were made of solid wood, not the rubber and foam hammers you might find in an earthly arcade, and 4) the heads were obviously in pain because, well, real heads, getting hammered with clubs, get hurt.

We stopped at the first "game." Arnold asked if the young man would mind stepping back a moment so we could speak to the heads getting whacked. "Not a bit," he replied. He put his club down and headed toward the snack bar.

The General gestured expansively. "This is the 'whack a politician' section of *Trump's Towering Inferno*, level six. Here we will see members of the House of Representatives who earned their place in Hell during their tenures before, during, or directly after Trump's term as president.

"It's clear why they are here: the world's greatest democracy. Humbug! What a joke. Republican members of Congress are bought and paid to do the bidding of the rich. They write their laws and cast their votes and take positions based not on what is best for the nation, but what was best for the billionaires and millionaires, the Republican Party, and themselves. Meanwhile, the nation is mired in scandals, looted by corrupt officials, and careens from one immoral, unsustainable, and counterproductive law or policy to another.

"It's true that many Democrats are in bed with big money too, but not to the extent the Republicans are.

"The men and women here profited handsomely by this system. Oh, sure, they were mostly small cogs in a big machine. Each was a member of a legislative body with 434 other members in the House of Representatives, so their voting impact was minor, but their positions were powerful. They personified destructive power that won them national attention, authority, fame, and influence. And did I mention money?

"Trump opened Pandora's Box and released these wretched beings on the nation and the world. His minions brought a maliciousness into the politics of this nation as bad as any in America's history. Day by day, session to session, press conference to press conference, these Congressmen and woman raced each other to the bottom. Every day, there was a contest to see who could say the most outrageous statement about guns, mask mandates, environmental degradation, racism. For instance, when the nation seemed to turn a corner on its racist history and traditions by electing its first black president, they helped give new life to racist individuals and organizations that made it open season again for hatred and bigotry. They gave Trump his opening and his first Big Lie, the birther myth that Barack Obama was not born in the United States and was therefore ineligible for the presidency.

"Trump became the figurehead and cheerleader for these ridiculous prats. He lied, distorted the truth, bullied. He made so many insensitive comments about so many different groups that he would have been fired from any other job in the country, from the manager of a fast-food restaurant to a public-school teacher or anything else.

"These representatives followed in lockstep. Then, they kept moving further into conspiracy theories and right-wing propaganda, following the crazy theories of Q-Anon, the insurrectionists, the anti-scientists, and those nitwit antivaxxers. They took many good-willed people in the United States down this road of ignorance, deception, and greed."

It all sounded about right, but Arnold was only warming up.

"You know what else?" he confided. "They were cruel. Imagine that. Servants of the people with enormous mean streaks. Like Trump, they attacked the poor, immigrants, minorities, Muslims, members of the LGBT community. They were mean and nasty. They found it to their advantage to create 'straw Democrats,' hypothetical political opponents with extreme positions that did not represent the party or any actual member of it, then attack those straw opponents with violent language. They exaggerated the positions of real Democrats, then attacked them for positions they did not support. And while this strategy got them elected and raised huge donations, it also served to further divide the nation and weaken the country from within."

We took the place of the young whack-a-mole player and stood in front of what looked like a medium-sized desk The horizontal top had a large, circular hole in the middle. After a moment, a head popped up out of it. The head belonged to a middle-aged man. His eyes were closed, and his shoulders drawn together around his neck. He was expecting a beating. His head was full of lumps, blood ran down his face from numerous cuts, his nose was broken, his lip split, and his eyes blackened.

"This is Representative Jim Jordan, former representative of Ohio's 4th Congressional district," the general said. "He, like others in this room, has been found guilty of lying to the American public and crimes again humanity. Just as he took swings against the truth during his time in Congress, so now will he be on the receiving end of blows from the wooden club you see here leaning against the table."

At this, Jordan disappeared again, below the surface.

"Each time a head pops up, the person who's "up" at the table gets to take one good shot at it. After that, the head retreats for an hour. This goes on all day, every day for eternity."

"Jim Jordan deserves this?" The whole thing seemed a bit extreme to me.

Arnold scoffed. "Jim Jordan! Jim was a traitor to all that he pretended to defend. He was a great athlete and wrestler, winning state titles in high school and national titles in college. After college, he worked for eight years as an assistant wrestling coach at Ohio State. This was during the time the university employed as the wrestling team's physician Richard Strauss, who sexually molested a reported 177 student athletes. Jordan, whose locker was next to Strauss's, consistently denied knowledge of Strass's criminal behavior despite repeatedly telling Strauss that if he 'tried anything like that on him Strauss would not get away with it.' Jordan refused to cooperate with the independent investigation of Strauss's sexual assault. Strauss died by suicide in 2005 as the details of his crimes were becoming public knowledge. Jordan's career took a different direction. He turned to politics. The political world is one where, if you can con enough people into pulling the lever or checking the box next to your name, you can be employed no matter what you have said or done.

"After his election to the U.S. House of Representatives, Jordan mastered the games of stonewalling and lying. He was a staunch ally of President Trump and said on Anderson Cooper in 2018, 'I don't know that [Trump has ever] said something wrong that he needs to apologize for,' and, when asked if he ever heard Trump tell a lie, said 'I have not' and 'nothing comes to mind.' Come on," the General said. "He actually said that! Trump never said anything he should apologize for and never lied! Give me a break! Jordan defended Trump in the first and second impeachment hearings. He's consistently denied global climate change, defended The Big Lie about the 2020 election, and done all he could to discredit Biden's win and democracy in the United States.

"Oh, and Jordan was always a promoter of easy access to every kind of gun. He actually proposed a waiting period . . . no, not the kind that slows a firearms purpose, but a statutory waiting period after every mass shooting during which legislators cannot pass any gun control laws, lest rights of gun owners be trampled out of sympathy for victims and survivors.

"When knowledge of what Jordan really knew about the sexual scandal at Ohio State finally became public in 2023, he continued to deny the evidence and facts, but soon thereafter lost his seat to another Republican in a primary. He went on to a pathetic career as a lobbyist for Big Oil, Big Guns, and the Big Lie. He appeared on Fox for a bit, but even they grew tired of his bollocks.

"His job here, getting pounded on this floor of *Trump's Towering Inferno*, is very secure. It's a no-brainer." The general smiled wryly. "Pardon the pun."

We watched the action at various tables, but as the top of the hour rolled around again, Arnold led me back over to the whack-a-mole game. When Jordan popped up again. Arnold hissed, "Traitor!"

Jordan's nostrils flared angrily as his face colored. "You," he said dismissively. "Look who's talking about traitors. I defended the Constitution. I fought for Americans' rights. I supported the greatest president in U.S. history. And for that I'm in lib-tard Hell?"

"No," Arnold replied. "You're in a Hell you and your cronies made for yourselves. You enabled a pedophile at Ohio State prey on young men when you did nothing to stop him, then lied about what you knew, causing further pain and more emotional damage for the victims. You took money for yourself and your campaigns from people who cared for nothing but themselves and certainly not the country. You supported positions you knew were popular with your constituents and would bring you fame and fortune but were bad for the nation and world. You backed Donald Trump before, during, and after his presidency despite knowing he was bad for the United States. Now you're receiving the wages of sin. Karma, as you Americans like to say, is a bitch. Like you, she has neither mercy nor sympathy."

Jordan sank back into his hole, but not before raising a middle finger over his head, so it was the last thing we saw as he disappeared. We moved on. The young man who had been playing returned with a drink in hand. He picked up the club and patiently watched the hole for Jordan's next appearance.

A few feet away was the next "whack-a-politician" station. This one was occupied by a young woman of about 20. She was carefully watching the hole in front of her.

Then, it happened. A head popped up. The young woman, club at the ready, wasted no time landing a baseball bat-like sideways jolt right above her politician's left ear. The beaten head's eyes rolled up as the head sank back into its hole. The young woman wiped sweat off her forehead and relaxed her posture.

"Who's being punished here?" I asked.

"Another whack job, a true dirt bag," Arnold replied. "That's Madison Cawthorn. Former representative from North Carolina.

"Cawthorn is linked to the other persons condemned to this level of Hell, and to all their cohorts in this building and others in different Hells around the world. What links them is their ability to lie. To manipulate facts and spin fiction as casually as if they were discussing the weather. Telling the Truth just does not appeal or apply to them they think. Maybe they started with small, harmless, white lies in childhood—who doesn't? But only a few can attain their level of proficiency, a state akin to pathological lying, saying anything that was intentionally deceitful and spurious. And as you know, when politicians lie, people's lives are affected. People are hurt, others die.

"Cawthorn lied about being accepted to the Naval Academy. He had been denied. He lied about being accepted to Princeton and an on-line program at Harvard. He was not. After a terrible accident that left him disabled, he lied about the details of the accident. He spent one semester at college, where he earned mostly grades of D and was credibly accused of sexual assault by multiple women. When he ran for Congress in 2020, more than 150 former students at that college signed a letter in which they accused him of being a sexual predator (Kranish, 2021).

"He lied about being a full-time staffer for Mark Meadows in 2015 and 2016, when Congressional records indicate that he was part-time, receiving $15,000 salary in 2015 and $5,000 in 2016 (Kranish, 2021).

"His election to the U.S. House of Representatives at age 25 is symptomatic of the failures of the Republican Party, specifically, and the United States, in general. This is what he had on his resume when he was elected to the House: a high school diploma (which he received from being home schooled), one semester of college where he received mostly grades of D, work at a Chick-fil-A, part-time work for Meadows, and a short-lived attempt as a real estate investor that provided him with no income.

"I ask you, is that a resume that qualifies anyone for election to the U.S. House of Representatives? Apparently, it is. But should it be?"

Before I had time to answer, Arnold continued.

"Since his election, Cawthorn has continued to promote a string of baseless conspiracy theories and lies. He was another gun-toting, race-baiting, up-and-coming Republican who posted a photo of himself at Adolf Hitler's vacation home, the Eagle's Nest, which he visited because it was 'on his bucket list.' Do you know anyone else who has Hitler's vacation home on their 'bucket list?'

"His campaign created a website for attacks on journalist Tom Fiedler, who had written articles critical of Cawthorn. The website said that Fiedler left the academic world 'to work for nonwhite males, like Corey Booker, who aims to ruin white males running for office.'

"He has told his colleagues that he seems himself not as a legislator, but as a messenger, writing, 'I have built my staff around comms [communications] rather than legislation.' A voracious spreader of conspiracy theories, he maintains The Big Lie and has 'prophesied' violence 'if our election systems continue to be rigged and continue to be stolen.'"

We moved ahead. Arnold pointed to another pop-up head as he leaned in confidentially. "Matthew Gaetz," he said. "It was never hard to see where he was going to be spending eternity, not from his earliest days in the House of Representatives. Everyone who ever met him or saw his photograph thought he looked like a cartoon criminal. It was only a matter of time before his life matched his physical image, and he wound up indicted and served at her majesty's pleasure. Oh, and wasn't he served! Sex with a minor. Interstate sex trafficking. Prostitution. Drugs. Corruption at the highest level. Another lowlife reaping what he sowed."

We watched an adolescent girl give Gaetz' head a foot-planted wallop with all her weight behind it. There might have been something personal in her attack. Matt Gaetz squeezed his eyes shut as his head disappeared into the table.

The fourth head in this "whack-a-politician" midway was Republican Representative Scott DesJarlais, who hailed from Tennessee. DesJarlais, a member of the Tea Party and a Trump supporter, sold himself as a staunch defender of family values and strongly prolife, even though his wife at the time had had two abortions, and a tape was discovered of DesJarlais and his wife imploring a woman with whom DesJarlais had an affair to go and get her own abortion. Under oath, DesJarlais testified that he had affairs with six different women while serving as chief of staff at the Grandview Medical Center in Jasper, Tennessee, including three coworkers, two patients, and the representative of a drug company. DesJarlais was considered by many to be the greatest hypocrite and worst low life in the House of Representatives. His personal behavior mirrored that of The Donald.

"Let's be clear," the general said. "People are people. To err is human. Both Democrats and Republicans make mistakes, do stupid stuff. The difference is that Democrats, at least at that point in time during the term of Donald Trump, cleaned up these messes while the Republicans did nothing. Think of Democrats Anthony Weiner, Al Franken, and Andrew Cuomo. These three men were credibly accused of sexual misconduct, sexual assault, and criminal behavior. They were criticized by Republican leaders, but that's not why they gave up their seats. They resigned because Democratic leaders would not allow them to stay in office.

"By contrast," he continued, "the Republican leaders look the other way when charges are brought against their colleagues. Their duplicity echoes through the subculture that supports them. Their silent, and not-so-silent, support of miscreants empowers others across the nation to do the same things. Tens of thousands of young men and women have been sexually assaulted because even the most casual observer can see that the perpetrator is unlikely to face any consequences for their actions.

"These four men, Jordan, Cawthorn, Gates, and DesJarlais are here for their hypocrisy, for their lies, for their part in or knowledge of sexual impropriety and limitless support of Donald Trump." He spat. "They disgust me."

We moved on, further away from the stairs, further into the arcade. A shooting gallery appeared in front of us. I followed Arnold into it.

I've been to many arcades in towns and cities across the United States. I've seen old arcades that have classical, mechanical games from days gone by, and new arcades with the latest electronic games and technology. I have seen arcades at amusement parks, at traveling state fairs, and others in malls or stores that are open year-round. I think most of these arcades have shooting galleries of some sort. Some of the shooting galleries are electronic, with rifles shooting digital bullets at pixelated villains. Other galleries have air guns, where targets are knocked over when "hit." Still others have guns that shoot tiny pellets at targets, knocking them over only to see the target stand up again as a conveyor cycles them around on a circuit.

This shooting gallery was like others outside *Trump's Towering Inferno*—but different. It had three stations for shooters, and they had rifles laying on the counter, facing the gallery.

This shooting gallery also had targets to shoot at. Targets moved lazily from left to right about 20 feet from the shooters, just like other shooting galleries.

But these targets were real people, at least as viewed from the shoulders up. These targets cringed and squinted as they moved down the row. I immediately recognized Marjorie Taylor Greene, the controversial representative from Georgia, on the conveyor. As she moved from left to right, the three players all took aim and fired.

Arnold shook his head as he indicated MTG. The United States has freedom of speech," Arnold stated. "You are free to believe and say whatever you want. But come on—I knew your so-called 'Founding Fathers,' and they never envisioned a nut-job like Greene addressing anyone except her fellow inmates in a madhouse. Instead, she became a leader of a powerful political party.

"She endorsed and spread many far-right conspiracy theories, too many to recount," he continued. "Among the worst were her anti-Semitic beliefs and the "white genocide" conspiracy theory she pushed. Maybe you've heard it called the white extinction or Great Replacement theory. Its proponents insist that there is a deliberate plot, usually blamed on Jews and persons of color, to make white people extinct. Greene was a true believer in Q-Anon, Pizzagate, antifa mass shootings, and Jewish lasers. Before she ran for Congress, she advocated the execution of Democratic politicians and compared the Democratic Party to Nazis for pushing safety policies related to COVID. And, of course, she chants The Big Lie like a mantra, claiming consistently that Trump won in a landslide and that the victory was stolen from him. She filed articles of impeachment against Joe Biden on January 21, 2021, the day after he took office, for abuse of power.

Marjorie Taylor Greene

"She made public claims that the 2017 Stoneman Douglas High School shooting in Parkland, Florida, as well as the Sandy Hook Elementary School in Connecticut shootings were faked 'to persuade the public to support strict gun control.' She called David Hogg, a survivor of the Parkland shooting and a gun control advocate '#littleHitler' and an 'idiot' who is trained 'like a dog.' She stalked Hogg multiple times, taunting him when he traveled to Washington, D.C., to speak to legislators about reasonable gun control laws.

For these reasons and oh-so-many more, she is one of the favorite targets here on Level Six."

At least one of the shooter's bullets found its target. Greene's head exploded into a gruesome spatter of blood, hair, skin, and bones.

As I watched, though, Greene's head began to regrow, expanding from the bottom like a slow-inflating balloon. Greene's face had just about returned to its normal size when it reached the edge of the shooting gallery and went out of sight. The shot to the head had hurt like Hell, though. Greene's eyes were puffy with tears, and her countenance screwed up in pain.

As Greene's head disappeared, another familiar face began drifting across the target zone in the shooting gallery. I could not place the name of the character, though. "Who is that?" I asked.

"Lauren Boebert." the general replied. "Another fanatical right-wing nutcase. She was one more member of the Republican Party in Congress who was elected just as Donald Trump was losing, but she rode into Congress with her crazy platform and the support of Trump voters in her district, which rallied around her ignorant and racist message.

"As you know, these are unusually crazy times. Boebert claimed that she became a 'born-again Christian' in 2009, yet her positions and policies reflect an anti-Christian worldview. She and her husband opened *Shooters Grill* in Rifle, Colorado, in 2013, where staff members are encouraged to carry their firearms openly while working. She claimed that she received her concealed carry permit for a gun after a man was 'beat to death by another man's hands . . . outside of [her] restaurant.' This claim was a lie. The man in question died about a block from her restaurant from a meth-amphetamine overdose after an altercation a few minutes earlier and a few blocks away.

"She maintained close ties with militia groups such as the Oath Keepers and Three Percenters and promoted herself as a gun-rights activist.

"So, as a general in the Continental Army, I carried and used weapons. I killed numerous soldiers from both the British and American sides. I also hunted," the general said. "I support what you call the Second Amendment, the modification to the U.S. Constitution that gives Americans the right to possess weapons (bear arms). But your defenders of the Second Amendment in your day are out of control. The Second Amendment was not given to America by God as a fundamental, inalienable right that could never be regulated or, for that matter, overturned." Arnold rolled his eyes.

"Yes, the Second Amendment gave individuals the right to own guns. And, yes, many Americans through the years have owned guns for hunting or to defend themselves. Then again, if you own a gun, you are eight times more likely to shoot someone in your family than a criminal who wants to enter your home. And an assault rifle, like an AR-15, or a machine pistol like a TEC-9, were never designed for hunting, but are weapons of war and should never be owned by private citizens of any nation.

"Republican legislators allowed for and even helped create an environment that led to the explosive number of guns being produced and purchased in the United States. These purchases helped fuel the individual and mass shootings in the United States in the 21st century. Not just to repeat a phrase or sound like a cliché, but they have actual blood on their hands. Innocent men, women, and children were shot and killed because of the likes of Lauren Boebert."

Boebert's face moved across the shooting field. The young shooters hustled back to their guns and took aim. Another hit, another head blown to pieces.

Just as Boebert's head slowly began to reform, another head began its trip across the shooting area. This was another gun-rights advocate and conservative extremist who stands somewhere to the right of Genghis Kahn on most issues, Paul Gosar. Gosar, from Arizona, is so controversial that six of his nine siblings have endorsed his opponents in congressional races.

Like many of his right-wing colleagues, Gosar has ties to white nationalist groups, is opposed to immigration, the Affordable Care Act, climate change, and, of course, gun control. A fierce defender of Trump, he boycotted the visit and address to Congress of Pope Francis. He was the only member of Congress to do so. He created a fundraising campaign based on his opposition to the Pope because the Pope would not speak out against violent Islam and Planned Parenthood, and because the Roman Catholic leader believes in and speaks in defense of global climate change.

Gosar was one of one of only 14 House Representative who voted against the Juneteenth holiday, defended the blatant racist comments of Steve King, spoke at a rally in London in support of anti-Islam activist Tommy Robinson, and lied by claiming that the white nationalist organization, Unite the Right, had been created by the left. He has claimed that members of the FBI and Department of Justice were traitors to the United States, and he has significant ties to extreme militia groups.

"Gosar's placement here is symbolic and representative

of his and others' dangerous policies of hatred, division, and racism that roiled the United States in the 2020s and beyond. They were flirting with, and even inviting, open armed insurrection against the United States and its democratically elected leaders. They feared that the liberals were 'taking over' and that racial and ethnic minorities would become the majority (which is a fact of demographics that has nothing to do with politics) and that whites would be marginalized, discriminated against, and even victims of blatant antiwhite genocide (decidedly not true). Gosar and his supporters focused on the Second Amendment, which reads, 'A well regulated Militia, being necessary to the security of a free State, the right of the people to keep and bear Arms shall not be infringed.' These extremists actually believed it was their right, and moral duty, to be prepared and ready to overthrow the United States government because it had moved too far to the left," the general stated.

I will spare you the details of Gosar's time in the gallery, simply noting that his experience mirrored that of Greene and Boebert. It was time to move on.

We moved to the center of the room. In front of us was the air hockey table I saw as we entered the room. Two young men were busy knocking a small, plastic puck back and forth across the surface. The puck had a face on it: it was the mug of Kevin McCarthy, who was being knocked back and forth with violent hits by the young men. It was a form of punishment I had never imagined before seeing it acted out right in front of me. But seeing was believing.

"Kevin McCarthy," said Arnold. I was prepared for another rant. "What was most noteworthy about the Republican Party during and following the Trump presidency was the rise of such notable daft and shameless liars as seen here in this level of *Trump's Towering Inferno*, and in the other levels above and below us. Think of the decline of the Republican Party, from Richard Nixon to Ronald Reagan, to Bush II and then Trump. What a descent!

"The Republican Party once stood for solid, conservative values. It stood for family values, fiscal responsibility and a balanced budget, support of the rule of law, police and governmental leaders, and a strong defense of democracy against communism and fascism, among other policies. Abraham Lincoln was a Republican! So was Theodore Roosevelt and Dwight Eisenhower, to name a few. But the Republican Party has lost its intellectual core and defining message. Think of the voices who left the party during the Trump years: Joe Scarborough, Steve Schmidt, Jennifer Rubin, Bill Kristol, Colin Powell, George Will, Max Boot, and Richard Painter. The list, of course, goes on and on.

"In their place are individuals who celebrate ignorance. Ignorance! They challenge scientifically accepted theories and research. The modern Republican Party members and their leaders believe multiple conspiracy theories and promote them to their base. Such stupidity and lack of intellectual integrity.

"McCarthy earned his way onto the air hockey table. No one ever accused McCarthy of being the brightest bulb in the room. His mediocrity and lack of a conscience was what made him the perfect Republican tool. The old joke about lawyers is that sometimes even lab rats won't do what they are asked to do. You cannot say that about Kevin McCarthy.

"An example of his intellectual acumen came in 2015 when he first announced his candidacy for Speaker of the House of Representatives as John Boehner was stepping down. During an interview on Fox News with Sean Hannity, Mc-

Carthy said, and here I paraphrase, that the Benghazi hearings were held to hurt Hillary Clinton's appeal and support and drive her approval ratings down rather than to get at the truth of what happened during that event. McCarthy's comments showed he was not yet ready for this leadership position. But he surfaced a few years later and was elected to the position of House minority leader.

"McCarthy is willing to say anything, anytime, and anywhere, as seen in his flip flopping on the presidential election results in 2020. Initially, he supported the Trump claims that the election had been stolen until the insurrection of January 6 and following days, when he temporarily flipped on Trump. We know what he was thinking because we have the tapes! But McCarthy reversed his field again, showing up in Mar-a-Lago a few weeks later, convinced that despite the codswallop that was Trump's presidency, the best way for the Republicans to win back the House of Representatives and Senate was through whole-hearted support of the former president. And, of course, if the Republicans gained enough seats in the House, McCarthy would have been the speaker of the House, a remarkable achievement for a man of limited intellectual ability but unlimited ambition and disregard for personal shame. He clearly aimed too high for his nut."

McCarthy's punishment on the game table continued. I noticed there were no openings, no slots for the puck to enter, no "goals" on this air hockey game. I asked Arnold why.

He explained, "There are no goals, no scoring in this arcade-like game, because there is no escape, no rest, no dropping out of sight for a moment for the pond scum McCarthy. He is snookered here with no escape."

We turned away. Arnold pointed to the staircase. I admit to

being relieved. How much more pain could Hell mete out to Trump and his MAGA pals?

As always, the General seemed to intuit what was on my mind. "This is Hell," he reminded me. "Everyone is here for what they did and their lack of remorse for doing it. They will get no relief because they deserve no relief. Put away your feelings of sympathy and compassion. Time to move forward."

With that, we said goodbye to another level of *Trump's Towering Inferno* and headed to the stairs.

CHAPTER 7

APPALLING ADVISORS

There once was a man named Trump
A narcissist, racist old grump
He lost an election
Incited an insurrection
But finally was kicked out on his rump.

We climbed the staircase in silence. Seriously, what do you say at such moments? "The weather has been nice recently?" No. "Did you catch the Yankees game last night?" Not going there. "How do you think the market will do in the coming months?" I don't think so. Silence was best.

We reached the next landing, and I saw another simple number announcing the floor: "7." We had reached level seven of *Trump's Towering Inferno*. Arnold grasped the doorknob and, turning his head toward me, asked "Ready, mate?" I took a deep breath and nodded. In we went.

I have learned that if you read about something in advance, you create a mental image of what you have read. When you see what you read about, it sometimes fits what you saw in your mind's eyes, and sometimes does not. Think of the Grand Canyon, for example: can anything really prepare you for your first sight of this incredible national park?

I will try to describe what I saw here. But it will be difficult. My writing skills are not worthy to describe what was before me.

As the door opened, I could see that we were in a large, dark cavern and that the main activity was taking place in the center of the room. I saw a huge living being that I recognized as "the Beast," that is, The Beast of Revelation 13. The Beast known by the number 666. John of Patmos described the beast as having seven heads. This seemed fanciful until I counted them: One, two, three . . . seven. Wow!

The Beast gnawed a human being in each horrible mouth. The men and women screamed in pain and terror as they were chewed on. The beast paid its victims' protests no heed whatsoever, biting as necessary and chewing slowly and carefully.

There was a faint stirring in the back of my mind. Didn't Dante describe this beast??

I glanced at the general. Once again, he was ready with a reply to my unspoken question.

"At the lowest level of Dante's *Inferno*, we find Satan. Dante portrays him as a three-headed monster, trapped in ice up to his waist. Dante imagined Satan as this three-headed monster to be the metaphorical opposite of the Trinity, God in the three persons of the Father, Son, and Holy Spirit. There, Satan also consists of three evil "persons." The three-headed Satan chews on the three greatest traitors of all time: Judas, in the middle mouth, Brutus, and Cassius on either side."

"It's enlightening to read Dante," the General suggested "He put a religious person, Judas, and two political persons, Brutus and Cassius, at the lowest level of his *Inferno*, thus showing divine interest in and divine punishment for religious and political offenders. For Dante, both social institutions are important. God is not interested just in religious affairs but also in what happens at the governmental level and real world.

"But this is not Dante. This is *Trump's Towering Inferno*. Here is The Beast of *Revelation*, the seven-headed beast John saw in a vision and described therein. The Beast is chewing on the men and women who advised Donald Trump and knew that he was delusional and demented. They knew he was irrational and unhinged, but they supported him nevertheless. They aided and abetted him. They assisted and encouraged him. The reign of Trump took place because these immoral men and women enabled his behavior. For this, they will be chewed on for eternity."

I wanted to cower by the stairwell. In fact, I wanted to leave altogether, to leave the building and return to my home in Connecticut, or back to that idyllic village in Mozambique. But Arnold bade me to move forward. I reluctantly followed.

"First, we see Kellyanne Conway. What a shame. She sold her unique talent for lying, deceiving, distorting, and detouring from the truth and used to it 1) help Donald Trump get elected as the president of the United States, and 2) serve for over three and a half years as one of Trump's senior advisors and 'go to' spokesperson. In her role as senior advisor, she alternated between defending and protecting whatever the president said or did no matter how inane or crass his words or actions, and attacking and confronting reporters, elected or appointed officials, and members of the public when they called out his behavior.

"She knew this was wrong. Her own husband, Republican attorney George Conway III, and her daughter, Claudia, repeatedly criticized the president and his behavior. George was the founder of the political action committee (PAC) called The Lincoln Project. One ad released by The Lincoln Project included these words by the video's narrator: 'Millions worry that a loved one won't survive COVID-19, there's mourning in America . . . . Under the leadership of Donald Trump, our country is weaker, and sicker, and poorer.'

"She used and elevated the phrase 'alternative facts' while appearing as a guest of Chuck Todd when defending Sean Spicer and the president regarding crowd size at his 2017 inauguration. She violated the Hatch Act by repeatedly expressing political positions while serving in public office, and she shamelessly promoted products sold by Ivanka Trump. She maintained that the COVID-19 virus was 'contained' in March 2020, as the virus was spreading like a wildfire across the nation. She defined the phrase 'kung-flu' as a racist dismissal of COVID-19 and dared reporters to identify which White House employee used such a phrase, only to stand by silently when Trump himself used it multiple times at the White House and while on the campaign trail.

"She was bad news. Bad for her family, bad for the Republican Party that fell into the Cult of Trump, bad for the United States, and bad for the world. She died a bitter old woman, divorced, disgraced, disowned, and estranged from her children. She was ushered immediately and directly to this level of Hell and into The Beast's mouth here in *Trump's Towering Inferno* with a unanimous verdict from the divine judgement panel. Arnold poked my upper arm and pointed toward the beast. "Go ahead, you can speak to her."

Another deep breath as I gathered my thought. "Ms. Conway, do you stand by your support of former president Donald Trump?" That seemed like a direct, simple, and easy-to-answer question.

Kellyanne mostly dodged a beastly incisor, which raked her forearm hard enough to draw blood. Peering at the gash, she winced before composing her face into a slightly bemused and condescending smirk. "Oh yes," she said. "Of course. I could have had any job in the Administration or private sector. I made my own millions doing market research for politicians and for women's magazines—if Courteous George thinks he's getting any of that money in the divorce settlement, he'd best read the fine print in the pre-nup! Anyway, I chose that role in Washington. *I chose that role!* Of course, Donald Trump was an idiot, an *enfant terrible*. He was always the least informed, least knowledgeable, least policy-interested person in the room. *Everyone* in the White House knew this. The staff, members of his cabinet, elected and appointed officials, religious and business leaders.

"But to serve him gave me a place in history and a seat at the most important table in the world. I knew I could run his campaign and give him a chance of winning and thus become the first woman to successfully run a presidential campaign. Nailed it! I knew I could serve as a senior advisor because I could outsmart, outmaneuver, and outtalk the press corps and do it *all* the time. I knew I could exchange my time in the White House for a lucrative book deal and other jobs that should have kept me fat and happy for the rest of my life. Sure, not everything turned out like I hoped, but I did what I did and have no regrets."

Arnold stepped in and faced me. "You see this woman? She is typical of everyone here in Trump's Hell. As you can see for yourself, she has no remorse, feels no guilt, no regrets, or apologies. She won't rot in Hell, nor burn here. Instead, she'll be chewed on by The Beast. Another just punishment. Ready to move forward?"

"I think so." If decades between The Beast's teeth was not enough to induce repentance, it was not going to happen during my visit.

"Very well." We moved forward 10 or 12 steps. The Beast was large!

"Here is what we like to refer to as the 'Stephen Section,'" Arnold explained. "It is also known as the 'Racist Corner.' Stephen Bannon and Stephen Miller. Racism run amok. Two blatant, overt, unashamed, and transparent racists whose personal ideologies dovetailed right into Trumpism. Like flies to manure, Trump attracted the worst of the worst of Americans to his cause, his campaign, and his administration. Here we find super-racists Stephen Bannon and Stephen Miller.

"Miller was, for all intents and purposes, the author of the child separation policy. This was the Trump Administration's policy put into place to detach the children of would-be immigrants to the United States from their parents at the Mexican border. Sometimes, this was accomplished by literally ripping the children out of their mother's or father's arms. The children were then placed in cages while their cases were being 'processed.' Often, their parents were sent back to their native countries without documenting the family relationship. This policy was established to discourage other parents from attempting to enter the United States.

"Bannon was proud of his racism, associating himself with Breitbart, the alt-right website that 'pushed racist, sexist, xenophobic and antisemitic material into the vein of the alternative right' (Elliot and Miller 2016). He was also banned from Twitter about the same time Trump was banned. Bannon was banned for suggesting that Anthony Fauci and Christopher Wray should be beheaded. Beheaded. Can you picture that? Come on, man. I mean, what distinguished Bannon ideologically from members of ISIS, the Taliban, and al Qaeda?

"Bannon accepted a pardon by President Trump for his conspiracy to commit mail fraud and money laundering. We don't even need to use the word 'alleged,' because to accept a pardon, by definition, means you were guilty. He paused for a beat. "Care to have a word with them," Arnold asked.

"Not really. Should I?"

"There's no point. They both believed they were superior to people of color, Muslims, Democrats, LGBT persons. Speaking to them only gives them another opportunity to spout their racist bunkum."

We continued walking around the edge of The Beast and came to the fourth individual suffering in the mouths of the brutish creature. It was Mike Pence. His face was as red as the red stripe of the American flag he wrapped himself in during his political career.

Mike Pence. Former vice president of the United States. One heartbeat away from the presidency. Among the things you could say about Pence was this: No one was convinced Trump should be impeached or otherwise removed from office because then the nation and world would have Mike Pence as president. Many thought he would be worse than Donald Trump. And that's saying a lot.

"Mike Pence ran one of the most unsuccessful campaigns for the presidency in history given his status as the former Vice President. Although he was able to raise millions of dollars, he was unable to receive support from more than five percent of the Republicans polled. He ended his campaign before any primary votes were even cast.

"Pence has this mantra that he repeated throughout his political career. It was 'I'm a Christian, a conservative, and a Republican—in that order.' Truth is, he was a cynical, manipulative politician first and foremost. He hid behind the shield of Christianity and being prolife to his position one heartbeat away from becoming the president of the United States.

"Had he been a true Christian, he would have stepped off the ticket when the Access Hollywood tape was released. Were he a conservative, he would have opposed the unprecedented growth of the national debt under the Trump administration and remained opposed to Trump's pandering to global dictators. Were he a Republican, he would have remained faithful to that political party and joined the never-Trumpers in ensuring this man never got close to the presidency."

"I'm ready to talk with the former Vice President," I said.

"Go for it."

"Mr. Pence. I have two questions for you. First, do you believe that slogan you developed and used throughout your political career, the one, 'I'm a Christian, a conservative, and a Republican—in that order?'"

"Of course not," he gasped, trying, desperately (and unsuccessfully) to ignore his pain and show he was fine. "I heard someone else say something similar when I was young. Another local politician used to say, 'I'm a Christian first, liberal second, and Democrat third.' I liked the sound of it and adapted it to my needs. After all," he said, pausing for a moment during which I think the Beast ground its teeth on this prisoner, then continued, "After all, I was from Indiana. There's lots of Christians there, and lots of conservatives. It's a Red State, for Christ's sake. So, I chose the Republican Party as my ride to the top. And I made it damn high—almost to the top, riding that phrase and always appearing to be Christian while advocating for self-serving programs and policies. I wanted to . . ."

I cut him off. "My second question is, why didn't you do more as the chairperson of the Coronavirus Task Force to help mitigate the pandemic and save American lives?"

"Well, that would have involved letting the American public know we had no plan, no policy, and no clue how to deal with this virus, and that that COVID-19 presented serious health dangers to the people. We could not do that. We had to pretend everything was just fine so that the economy would remain strong, and we could win a second term. Then, once Trump completed his second term, his eight years, I would slide right in behind him and assume the mantle of the world's most powerful person.

"Of course, there was always the possibility that the president might be impeached again, or that he might resign or die in office. Those options were all possible, although Trump resigning never seemed realistic. But I was hopeful. You know the old phrase, 'keep your friends close and your enemies closer.' For four years, I was the bobble-headed doll that shook my head yes to everything Trump said and said no to every person or group in opposition. It was easy for me as a two-faced hypocrite. Before the vice-presidency, I was fast approaching' has-been' status. Trump elevated me and made me important. I gave him Christian creds. I am grateful to him, my lord and leader."

I could not read Arnold's face. I thought I saw signs of anger, frustration, and disgust. But mostly, I think, resignation if not indifference.

A silent glance passed between us and the general and I moved forward. A few steps more took us to a partially consumed Rudy Giuliani. Known once as "America's Mayor" after the 9/11 attacks in New York City, the nation watched his decline and fall during the succeeding 20 years. He died disbarred, disgraced, and dishonored a few years after being fired by Donald Trump himself for his failure to overturn the presidential election loss of 2020.

"There are waaaaaaaay too many stupid things Giuliani said or did to review here," the general said. "Suffice it to say he really was an arsehole who had one incredible hot streak during the days and weeks after 9/11. He rose to that occasion, but soon slipped back down to the gutter from which he had come and, during his time with Trump, ran right out of the gutter and into the sewer. During Trump's campaign in 2016, Giuliani defended Trump against allegations of racism, not paying federal income taxes for almost 20 years, and sexual assault. For his early and consistent support of Trump, it was rumored that Giuliani would be named Trump's Secretary of State. Thank God, or someone, that never happened. Instead, he was hired as Trump's personal lawyer, for which lying was a prerequisite, something Rudy had no trouble doing.

"As Trump's personal attorney, Giuliani defended the indefensible. We all know that attorneys have been known to spin the truth, to bend reality and cherry-pick facts that support their arguments. But Giuliani did not stop there. Among other things, he got involved in the Stormy Daniels affair, defended the president during his impeachment trials, traveled to Ukraine to dig up dirt against Joe Biden, contested the 2020 presidential election with a series of legal motions based on false information and lies, and empowered the mob on January 6 by using the phrase 'trial by combat.'" The General glanced over, his lips pressed together in disgust. "So, would you like to speak to this douchebag?"

"Is there any point to that?"

"Not unless he knows something you want to know. Even

Rudy Giuliani

under oath, he'll just keep spinning and yakking and digging deeper and deeper. That's what he has done since being assigned here. We think he lost his mind soon after his term as the mayor of New York ended in 2001. It just took some time for the rest of the nation to understand that he was suffering from mental health issues. He was just another dupe used by Trump, but of course, used willingly. Giuliani loved the limelight, loved being in and around the White House and U.S. Capitol. Loved being interviewed on Fox and

CNN and any other platform. He was eager to be on-camera in *Borat 2*. Remember that? Rudy thought he was about to have sex with an underage reporter from Kazakhstan. He is completely shameless. He's an embarrassment to residents of New York City and the United States. And, among politicians and lawyers, the status of 'embarrassment' is not easy to achieve."

I suddenly realized I had at least one question.

"Mr. Giuliani," I asked, "why are you here?"

America's Mayor opened his eyes, which had been tightly closed in pain. Between groans, he said, "They don't know what they are doing. I should be in Heaven. I have been misunderstood, misjudged, and mistakenly placed here. I have an appeal pending, though. I'm going over the head of St. Peter and his Pearly Gates judgement concession. Gonna reach out to the Big Guy Himself. I'll win this one on appeal. You'll see me in Heaven one of these fine days. They are not going to get away with this fraud forever. I deserve better, and by God – ha! – I'll get it!"

"But you told so many lies about everything since being named Trump's lawyer, culminating in your lies about the stolen election and the events leading up to the insurrection at the U.S. Capitol. You caused great harm to this nation. You amplified The Big Lie and reinforced the crazy conspiracy theories that are still influencing millions of Americans."

"I had the evidence for everything I said, believe me. Boxes of transcripts from depositions I took proving electing fraud. I documented hundreds of thousands of illegal votes that had been cast for Joe Biden. We were protecting democracy. At least, that is what we were pretending to do." He smiled lopsidedly. "I'm lying, of course. I don't have any evidence of voter fraud at all, much less evidence of MAS-SIVE fraud. Yes, of course, we knew Biden won. But here's the thing: By attacking our opponents and the Democrats and liberals, I kept my job, my profile, and stayed in the limelight. At least for a little longer. It was good for me, good for Trump, and good for the United States. The ends always justify the means, I don't care what anyone else says. I would do it again, take the whole bumpy ride. Well, maybe not the Four Seasons mess. But I should be transferred directly to Heaven, where I belong."

Um, no. Giuliani was in the right place too. Next stop—Mike Pompeo.

"You have no idea how many Trump advisors we had to consider for these seven mouths of The Beast," Arnold stated. "It was difficult to narrow it down to just seven. Too bad 'The Beast' was not a 50-headed monster. We still would have had a waiting list. Anyway, Pompeo. Another self-centered piece of dung who fell out of someone's arsehole. He would not have found himself in The Beast's jaws had he not served as Trump's Secretary of State, but in that role, he did great damage to the U.S.A., the high office he held, and himself. Some of the greatest names in U.S. history served in that position and being the secretary of state was once considered a steppingstone to the presidency. In fact, Trump's people feared that Pompeo considered himself presidential timber. If so, weighing his resume against Trump's, you could understand his thinking. He graduated number one in his class at West Point and served in the army for five years. He graduated from Harvard Law School, ran a profitable business, and was elected as a U.S. Representative in 2011. Initially, he opposed Donald Trump as his party's nominee. He even labeled Trump an 'authoritarian.' But after Trump won the nomination, Pompeo changed his tune and sang Trump's praises. Pompeo became one of his more vocal supporters. His sycophancy earned him, first, directorship of the CIA in January 2016. Then he was elevated to Secretary of State and sworn in after his 2018 confirmation.

"Pompeo lied like the rest of them. He lied about his knowledge and involvement in the impeachment trials of Trump. He lied about the COVID-19 pandemic. He authorized and announced an 'emergency' $8.1 billion (yes, with a B) arms sale to Saudi Arabia and the United Arab Emirates in 2019, knowing full well that American weapons had been used in a devastating war in Yemen that led to thousands of civilian deaths. He held mask-less parties, in violation of health policies and Washington, D.C., regulations. He was clearly gathering his own power base for a presidential run.

"When asked about the election results of 2020, Pompeo said 'there will be a smooth transition to a second Trump administration.' Following the insurrection of January 6, 2021, he tweeted that Trump should be considered for the Nobel Peace Prize. He made controversial and far-right policies and decisions right up to his final day in office." The general swung his head. "What a jerk."

"Can I ask him a few policy questions?"

"Far be it from me to stop you."

"Secretary Pompeo," I began, "in your role as the head of the State Department, you negotiated a timeline with the Taliban for removing American troops from Afghanistan and agreed to their demand that Afghanistan's government release 5,000 Taliban prisoners, some of them hardened criminals and known terrorists. But then, when the Biden administration followed through with the withdrawal of U.S. troops, you claimed you had nothing to do with the Trump deal and were against it. Can you explain this turnaround?"

"It was no turnaround," Pompeo said. He winced at a nibble from The Beast. "It was a calculated political move. I saw how Trump smoothly moved away from positions that had become unpopular. I saw how badly the final days of Biden's withdrawal went, and, considering my own aspirations, weighed in, giving myself the best scenario for future political office."

"You seem to think a lot about your own political interests, but did you like working for Donald Trump? What was your impression of him?"

"Donald Trump was an ignoramus. 'Stable genius' my ass. Tillerson had it right when he called him a 'fucking moron.' Trump asked Pence once if we could use nukes to stop hurricanes. He had no understanding of the U.S. Constitution—I doubt if he ever read it. He believed he knew more than the generals about warfare, more than the doctors about medicine, and more than the scientists about the global climate change. We defended him because we were afraid of falling on his bad side. We coveted his voter base."

"Did you think you might become president of the United States?"

"You bet I did. The power. The glory. The prestige and legacy. Yes, I wanted to be the president of the United States. I sought that position for decades and saw supporting Trump as a way of reaching my goal."

"But" I said, "You were on the wrong side of every ethical issue. Global climate change. Sexual identity. Health care. International criminal courts. The Iranian nuclear deal. International relations scholars Drezner, Sokolsky, and Miller described you as the worst secretary of state in American history (Sokolsky, 2019). Every time you spoke on an issue, you took the red-necked, knee-jerk reaction, inflaming the culture wars and further dividing the nation."

"Where's the beef?" Pompeo asked. "Politicians assess the situation they are in and make strategic decisions based on what will serve their political aspirations. I was smart enough to hitch my wagon to Trump. I knew his base was loyal to a right-wing agenda. So, I made the decision that this was my route to success. I took it. I miscalculated. It happens. But I was able to make a fortune in the arms industry and retired as a billionaire. I did just fine."

"Except you are in Trump's Hell," I pointed out.

"There is that. Still, my name is in the history books as Secretary of State. I left my family billions of dollars. I did what I thought was best for myself and family. If Giuliani can have hope, so can I. God will one day overturn this conviction and I will rise to Heaven. Mark my words!"

"Time to move on," the general suggested.

We rotated almost back to the front side of The Beast to visit the final Trump advisor caught up in its jaws. I was surprised to see Dr. Deborah Birx. "Dr. Birx?" I asked Arnold. "Really?"

"Sure. She fits. In her role as the White House Coronavirus Response Coordinator, her tepid and mixed messaging led directly to the death of over 800,000 individuals. In the biblical book of Revelation, we read 'I know your works; you are neither cold nor hot. I wish that you were either cold or hot. So, because you are lukewarm, and neither cold nor hot, I am about to spit you out of my mouth' (NRSV, 1991; Revelation 3:15–16). She waffled; people died.

"Remember that press conference where Trump suggested

using light or disinfectant to kill the virus? She squirmed a bit, and looked like a deer caught in the headlights, but she said nothing. I repeat, she said NOTHING! Nothing that day, or the next, or following week or month. Her silence was deafening. She played the virus down the middle, downplaying its deadliness while 'suggesting' social distancing and mask-wearing."

The General paused. He slowly shook his head and muttered something under his breathe, then continued.

"In April, 2019, she was the lead medical expert in the White House when public statements were released from the White House claiming that the virus had peaked and was quickly fading when, in fact, infections surged from then until early 2021, nearly two years later (Shear, 2020). She knew the real facts and data. In March 2021, after the Trump presidency had ended, she told Dr. Sanjay Gupta on CNN, 'Well, I look at it this way. The first time, we have an excuse. There were about 100,000 deaths that came from that original surge. All of the rest of them, in my mind, could have been mitigated or decreased substantially' (Wang, 2021). She told the world that all the deaths after the first 100,000 could be laid at the feet of the Trump administration, in which she was the health expert, the person Mike Pence called the 'right arm' of the task force. For her role, for her silence, here she is. Case closed."

"Wow. I'd like to ask her a couple of questions."

"Be my guest."

"Dr. Birx," I said as I approached her. "I have to ask: Are you sorry for your role on the White House Virus Task Force?"

She struggled to speak. About half of her was in the maw of The Beast. Her pain must have been terrible.

"I was not sorry for agreeing to be on the task force," she managed. "I should have spoken out more aggressively. Listen, you can't understand what it's like to work under Trump. He threatened us, bullied us, mocked, and ridiculed any ideas that were contrary to his. I so wanted to speak out, but I was afraid. I thought that keeping my position on that team was more important to the nation than getting kicked off and replaced by someone worse. So, while I softened my message, I prayed that the American public would understand and get enough other information from medical experts that they would ignore the President. My friend Fauci repeatedly encouraged me to be more vocal. I made a grave mistake. I am SO sorry. I screwed up. Can you tell the world I am sorry and ask for forgiveness?"

She had no sooner spoken than a small team of Capitol Hill police officers moved in. One jumped on the back of this seventh head of The Beast and administered an injection. When the head began to relax and wobble a bit, I saw the other police officers move in to rescue Birx from The Beast's maw. Birx's legs were smeared with blood. The police placed her on a hospital gurney and rushed her out of the room. Another group of police officers dragged a new morsel toward The Beast. I could not identify this individual.

I asked the General, "What just happened?"

"So, Dante got a few things right. He stated in his *Inferno* that Hell was for those who could not see their behavior as wrong, who could not acknowledge their sins and repent and ask for forgiveness. The guardians wait on the sidelines for any sign of repentance. They have been keeping a close eye on Dr. Birx for some time, thinking she knew her culpability in the spread of COVID-19 all along. You see they were right. Today, for the first time, they, and you, were able to see this yourself, witnessed her repentance. Hell is for the blind and not for those who see. While she deserved Hell, there is divine forgiveness. She will be reassigned."

"Where will she go?"

"Further down the road on her journey."

"Will she be released from *Trump's Towering Inferno*?"

"It's hard to say. I don't know. I know that she has been freed from The Beast's jaws. I know her case is being reviewed. Anything beyond that is above my paygrade, as you would say."

Meanwhile, Dr. Birx' replacement for the seventh mouth of The Beast began to scream and struggle to free himself. The screaming awakened the sleepy seventh head, which saw its next victim, and sprang into action. Its hideous neck extended, and it took a giant bite, pulling the man in to from the waist, with his head sticking out. The Beast began chewing. The man caught in its jaws began screaming in pain and terror. The police officers backed away, then turned and exited through the same door Dr. Birx had been taken.

"Who did they give to The Beast?"

"Dr. Scott Atlas. Another quack. He was next in line." Arnold took a step toward the staircase. "Ready to go? I think you have seen enough here." More than enough. I nodded. And with that, we were finished our tour of the seventh floor.

CHAPTER 8

FAMILY FEUD

Hickory dickery dock
Donald Trump was not a good pop.
He pushed his kin to win, win, win
But never discussed evil and sin.

The Trump Gang

As we climbed to the eighth floor, I thought, this would be a good time to ask the General about his defection during the Revolutionary War and his ensuing battles against the revolutionary troops he had fought alongside and led for five years. His decision and subsequent behavior are what gave him the label of being the most notorious traitor in America and among the worst in world history. So, was he that? How did his behavior look to him now? I concluded that neither I, or anyone else, might have the opportunity to ask Arnold about this, face-to-face. *Carpe diem.*

"So, General Arnold," I said, "you were a faithful and courageous general and leader of the American Revolution. You fought bravely, brilliantly, and sacrificially. You were wounded many times and contributed enormous amounts of your own money for your troop's supplies—a quarter million dollars in today's money. You were friends with George Washington and many other generals and revolutionary leaders. What made you switch sides? Why did you become a traitor to all you fought for?"

Arnold sighed. "Life's complicated, my friend. Nuanced, many shades of gray. Humans think in terms of black and white, but it is more complicated than that. The short answer to your difficult question is this: I grew weary of the fight. I lost heart. I was not the only one. I saw morale waning in both the armed forces and general population. The war dragged on with no end in sight. We were, and had been, British citizens after all. Our colonies were founded and established under the crown. We spoke *English*, used the British pound, and had been loyal to our mother nation for well over a century. So, once I lost confidence that England could be beaten into admitting that America could be an independent nation, I wanted back in her good graces. My "treason" just seemed like the right and natural thing to do. I was not promised, nor did I ever receive, any '30 pieces of silver,' nor a huge bribe or large payment. I earned a general's salary in the British army and a pension, but nothing more."

Here, I thought, Arnold bent the truth; he had been promised a large sum for allowing the British to take West Point, although that payment was never made because the scheme was foiled before it could be implemented. "Did you ever regret that decision?"

A long pause followed that query. Finally, an answer: "Every day," was his response.

"What was it like fighting for the British against American troops, in America?"

"Well, it was very strange, of course. The British moved me first to Virginia, where I led a raid against Richmond. We were successful in capturing that city and then went on a military campaign through the countryside destroying houses, foundries, and mills where the Americans were storing supplies for the Continental Army. We were trying to break the heart and morale of the American people.

"I made plenty of enemies. Thomas Jefferson promised anyone a £5,000 reward for my capture. George Washington sent orders to Lafayette, who was in Virginia at the time, to hang me, were I to be captured. The marquis refused to meet with me and returned my letters unopened, and when I asked one of Lafayette's aides what would happen to me had I been captured, he replied, 'We should cut off the leg which was wounded in the country's service, and we should hang the rest of you'" (Unger, 2002: 141).

"It was clear to me that many of the British soldiers under my command did not trust me. I returned to New York and petitioned General Clinton with a series of locations where I could be useful. I think he had also lost confidence in me, but he eventually relented and allowed me to lead a force of 1,700 soldiers against New London, Connecticut. I knew this area well because it was only a few miles from where I was born and raised.

"In Connecticut, we were successful meeting our military objectives, but I was met with opposition on both sides. We burned New London to the ground and burned many American ships that were anchored in that harbor and being used against us. We were also able to capture Fort Griswold, in Groton, Connecticut," he added.

"I led these battles. When the American soldiers surrendered after the Battle of Groton Heights, our troops slaughtered many of them. I was a few miles away attempting to coordinate the various components of the battle when I learned of the massacre. It was, in my mind, a shame, another tragedy in this war. But we in the military do not speak of such issues. We moved forward. I returned to New York and learned of General Cornwallis's surrender at York to Washington. Cornwallis was an idiot. I warned him that he had chosen a poor location to defend and encouraged him to establish a base further from the coast. I was ignored. It was clear I could not offer any more help to the British, and hence my role in the American Revolution came to end. I departed for England a few months later in December 1781."

"Following your attack in New London and Groton, the civilians of Norwich set fire to your family home, dug up your father's remains and threw them, along with his tombstone, into the Yantic River, which flows right by the cemetery and near your family home. How did that make you feel?"

"Terrible. Ashamed. Embarrassed. I spent the rest of my life considering what I had done and was filled with regret and remorse. But, living in London, I only shared my feelings with my closest family members and the local priest, all of whom I swore to secrecy. My job here in *Trump's Towering Inferno*, showing you the suffering of the men and women being punished here, is part of my own penance."

I nodded. "And tomorrow?"

"This is eternity. There isn't any 'tomorrow.' So, in some ways, same as you: Soldier on. Forward. But in other ways, it's different. Nobody sleeps in eternity, so I'll be doing whatever they need until my debt is settled and I'm released."

We arrived at the landing for the eighth floor. Time to return to this towering Hell.

Arnold opened the door. We walked through the threshold and found ourselves miraculously transported to an extremely poor section of a city in what was clearly a developing nation. I had been to many such locations in my life, but I was unsure where we were at this point. The signs on the stores and streets were in Arabic. The heat, low humidity, and dust made me think we were somewhere in the Middle East. "Where are we?" I asked Arnold.

"Gaza."

Gaza, I thought. What in the world are we doing here?

Quick search of Gaza memories. Or is it the Gaza Strip? I know the Gaza Strip is a thin piece of land running north to south between Israel and the Mediterranean Sea. I think it borders Egypt to the south and is separated from the rest of the Palestinian territory, the West Bank, by the state of Israel. But I could not for the life of me imagine why we were here.

"The Gaza Strip is one of the poorest and most overcrowded pieces of land in the world. Its people suffer from food, water, medicine, and power shortages. Over half of its people live in poverty. The region suffered from the Israeli military operations in 2008, 2014, 2018, and 2021 that greatly damaged civilian infrastructure and caused heavy casualties. A 14-year siege and blockade against Gaza by the Israelis has crippled the economic activities of this coastal region, leaving it at the point of a humanitarian crisis."

"So, why are we here?"

"This is the eighth level of *Trump's Towering Inferno*. Here we will visit the next group sentenced to Hell."

"OK." I said OK but my head was exploding with questions. How did we get to Gaza? What is going on? Is the tour of *Trump's Towering Inferno* over? Who might we find condemned to Gaza, of all places? I decided the last question was the best to ask. "Who will we find here?

"This is the level reserved for Trump's immediate family members. The worst of the worst. The bottom drawer. The lowest, scummiest, most immoral, obnoxious, revolting, and disgusting members of the Trump family. This level has been booked for them."

"What?" It was the best I could manage. "Why here, for them?"

"This is where Trump's family members will be for eternity, in the abject poverty they so neglected to notice or relieve in their lifetimes. Their carelessness—indeed, indifference—to the suffering of the world's people, their personal love of money and extravagant lifestyles and their positions of power within their dad's family and administration have condemned them to the punishment of walking the streets of the Gaza Strip as hopeless and homeless beggars. They will be here for eternity. It is another just penalty."

He pointed down the unpaved street. "Let's go," he said.

We walked together for about a quarter mile before turning left onto a narrow side street. Raw sewage mingled with garbage flowed in the gutter. Men, women, and children, dressed in old, dirty, and inexpensive clothing, moved through the streets in all directions as they went on their way to and from work, family, school, or other activities. Some carried food or packages. Despite their obvious poverty, they seemed happy and relaxed, as if moving to a nice location nearby.

Then, I saw him. Even in this foreign environment and in his miserable condition, I recognized him. Donald Trump, Jr. Deep breath. One step at a time, we approached this sorry spectacle of a person, slumped on the ground against a wall with a torn shirt and ragged pants. His face was sunburned, his feet unshod. His body was emaciated. An old pair of crutches lay by his side, along with an upturned cap for donations and a sign saying, "Unemployed Veteran: Help."

Arnold approached him and squatted down right in front of junior. He motioned for me to do the same. Having done so, the general encouraged me to speak with Donnie.

"Um, Mr. Trump. Why are you here?"

"I have no fucking idea! Where the Hell are we? I don't even know. These goddam idiots don't know who I am or even speak English. *I did nothing wrong in my life*! I had some fun, sure. I screwed lots of women—what's wrong with that? I drank some, did some coke, partied, sure. But I repeat: *I did nothing wrong.*"

Donnie leaned forward. "Can you get me out of here? I can pay you. My dad was a billionaire, you know. Elected and served a term as the president of the United States. Won a second term that was stolen from him. He and I pinched millions of dollars from the government, Republican National Party, friends, colleagues. We stashed it in banks, safe deposit boxes, and invested in offshore stocks and bonds. I can pay you."

"Why do you have a sign that says, 'Unemployed Veteran: Help?' You weren't a veteran. And the sign is in English. They don't read English here in the Gaza Strip."

"We're in the Gaza Strip? Really? No wonder there are so many fucking Muslims around. I thought maybe we were in Detroit. Get me the Hell out of here!" I gave him a sharp glance; the irony of his comments was lost on him.

He struggled to stand, using his crutches for support and balance. The general and I stood and backed away a step or two. Once up, Donnie came toward me, slowly and awkwardly, limping and moving poorly with the crutches. His face was red and his disposition threatening.

"Get me the Hell out of here!" he repeated, "Do you know who I am?" he screamed.

Arnold put up a hand. "Calm down, Donnie boy," he said, "calm down. My friend came here to speak to you. He has no ability or power to take you anywhere. He had nothing to do with your being here—that's on you. So why don't you sit down again and relax? Tell him your story, plead you case, and let the Heavens affirm your guilt, or set you free."

Donnie paid the general no heed. His face remained contorted with rage. He took another stumbling step toward us.

Then, he collapsed, falling like the proverbial potato sack. Down went Donnie.

Instinctively, I stepped forward to help, but the general blocked my way. He himself bent down on one knee and helped position Donnie back to where we had found him, sitting with his back against the wall. Donnie was subdued and groggy. After a moment, he roused. He shook his head to clear it, then began his lament again, his tone low but still angry.

"I am Donald Trump Junior. I was faithful to my father, who God personally chose to be the 45th president of the United States, and to our beloved flag, for which we stand. I helped my father make the nation great again during those years. My sister thought she would be America's sweetheart, the real First Lady," he laughed bitterly. "And yeah, I know how creepy that sounds, but you know how Dad doted on her, hell, wanted to date her, right? But she didn't understand Americans like I did. They don't want to idolize some rich-bitch sophisticate." He pronounced the word "SO-fist-eye-cate, drawing out the syllables and affecting a drawl. "No, they want a redneck gun nut they can relate to, and by God . . ." Junior hesitated and looked up as if expecting lightning. After a moment, he shrugged. "By God, I became that red-neck gun nut. Do you have any idea how hard I had to work at that? Transforming myself from a snooty, entitled prep-py kid to a snotty, entitled blue-collar dude? Have you ever tried going from Larry Summers to Larry the Cable Guy? Daniel Day Lewis couldn't pull off that acting job, but ol' Donnie, he did," he snorted. "I blew Ivanka off the stage, man, and took my place next to Dad.

"I stood with him and did everything in my power to over-turn the 2020 election that had been stolen from him, helped him try to win again when he ran in 2024, and did my best to follow in his footsteps in my own campaigns for the presidency after he died in 2025. I should be at his side in Heaven, not wherever the Hell we are now." He raised his eyes toward the sky and shouted, "*Get me out of this shithole!*"

The General nodded sorrowfully and looked away, down the street. I had learned by now that when he thought our time in any location was finished and there was nothing else to be gained, he moved us forward. We turned and began walking away. This infuriated Donnie, who yelled after us, hurling curses. I could make out these words: "It was all Ivanka and Jared's fault. They threw me and my father under the bus. They only cared about their place in society and having the media portray them as the 'reasonable ones,' even though they aren't any more reasonable than dad, me, Eric, or my buds down at the pistol range. They were a distraction. If we had all stayed on that train together, there'd be no stopping us. Hell, Barron would be president now." He hesitated. "Is he? That little half-breed bastard." He continued his angry tirade, but it was fading as we moved further away. We turned the corner and continued down the narrow alley.

We walked in thoughtful silence. One hundred, two hundred yards. We passed shops, homes, markets, and more. Disorientated and lost, I clung close to the general's side.

"There's no point going through the list of Donnie's lies, half-truths, and misleading statements. His focus on The Big Lie itself was enough. He clung to that to the end of his days. His ceaseless repetition of that ridiculous claim led to so much anger, hatred, destruction, and death in the United States," he sighed. "At last, he became the one of the most hated men in America. Even his dad's base began to see through him. That's the best thing that happened to America in the wake of his dad's decline and death.

"Look ahead. Do you recognize her?"

I could not place the rag-picker with her shopping cart.

"That's Kimberly Guilfoyle. She was Donnie's second wife. That marriage lasted just under a year. The rumors that she beat the tar out of Donnie were partially true. They got into several physical altercations. Though Kimberly got in a few shots, Donnie, who's 10 years younger, always managed to gain the upper hand and deliver his blows where no one could see the bruises and damage. She earned her nickname as 'Donnie beater' by attacking him one night with a baseball bat while he was asleep. That's when she gave him the concussion and broke his jaw and four ribs that was reported so widely in the press.

"She would have done better had she stayed married to her first husband, Gavin Newsome. As you know, his star continued to rise all the way to the top. Or her second husband, Eric Villency. Villency did not have the political ambition or chops Gavin, or Donnie did, but he was richer than either and on his way to the billionaire club. She should have stayed with Newsome or Villency. She was an idiot.

"She'll always be remembered for her shrieking rant at the Republican National Convention in 2020 when she concluded with that delusional line, 'The best is yet to come!' Look at her now. Like the rest of them, how the mighty have fallen."

"Should we speak with her?"

Arnold shook his head. "No. No point wasting our time with that political gold-digger."

We kept walking. Not far away we came to another sad look-ing beggar, can in hand, looking for donations. It was Eric Trump. At least, it appeared to be Eric Trump.

Slumped over, the thin elderly man wore an old, dirty hat, ragged shirt and pants, and, like his brother, was barefooted.

As we approached him, he jiggled his can. He knew we were in front of him but avoided eye contact by looking down at his feet.

"Salaam Alaikum," Arnold said, the traditional Muslim greeting translated as *peace to you*. Having lived in the Mid-dle East, I knew the expected response, *Alaikum Salaam*. Eric did not respond and kept looking at his feet, which for the first time I noticed were red and swollen.

"Don't you greet me when I greet you?" Arnold asked.

"I didn't understand you," came Eric's reply. "I speak En-glish. I have never understood the gibberish they speak here. Will you give me some change so I can buy some food? I am starving and have not eaten in several days."

"Do you know where you are?"

"No, I don't. If I had to guess, I might say the Middle East. Maybe Saudi, where my dad and our family did so much business. It was easy money. The royal family had soooooooooo much money and were so willing to spend it in ways to get close to my family and to Americans. It was the only place in the world where I could show a positive balance sheet, as my dad was always quick to remind me. Many of the men here are wearing robes and the women head coverings and they are all speaking a language similar to what I heard in Saudi—maybe it is the language Islam. So, I would say, likely we are in Saudi Arabia."

"Islamic language," Arnold scoffed. "You are an idiot. There is no 'Islamic language.' Its Arabic, you daft prat. You are in the Gaza Strip. You are here for all eternity on account of your crimes against humanity. You played a role in your father's administration and let him pretend he wasn't doing business while in the White House. You abused power, wealth, and influence throughout your lifetime, and you showed blatant disregard, nay, contempt, for the poor of your nation and those around the world."

"You mean, I have to stay here longer?"

"Yes, for eternity. You were told this when you were brought here years ago. Don't pretend you've forgotten."

"I kinda remember, but I thought that was some kind of a joke my dad was playing on me. He was always talking about wanting me to be a winner and what would happen if I failed or lost money or a deal fell through. I thought this was his way of letting me know I had misplaced another $10 million in some deal that went south."

I noticed for the first time that Eric had many missing teeth, and his gums were red and swollen around the teeth he retained.

"His teeth are abscessed or missing," Arnold whispered to me. "He can't remember to brush them, much less know where he is or why he is here. I wasn't insulting him earlier. He really is an idiot."

Apparently, he had not lost all his memory, because Eric suddenly frowned and asked, "Is my brother around? I'd like to get my hands on him. He betrayed me, you know. He thought he was dad's favorite. Thought he was the best spokesperson for our family. Always pushing me and my sisters aside. Of course, pushing Ivanka and Tiffany aside made sense. Don't get me started on Jared. And our half-brother Barron. They were all rotten. But I did nothing wrong. This joke isn't funny. I want to go home, back to my dad's tower in New York. I want to be recognized and treated right." His eyes pleaded with us. "C'mon. I get it. Let's call this a day. This is a terrible joke—I feel like I am in a living Hell."

No, he didn't get it. He had no clue.

Alone. Hurting, internally and externally. For eternity.

"You are in Hell, Eric. Let that sink into your limited brain. You will stay here forever." Arnold was firm. The dull light in Eric's eyes dimmed even more. He was beginning to understand his place in the universe, and it was not a good place to be!

"Let's keep moving," the general suggested. "We have others to see."

We walked away in silence. Eric returned to looking at his feet, weakly shaking his can of coins. We turned another corner and walked maybe a hundred yards. Ahead we saw an old woman sitting on a park bench. She was instantly recognized. Gone were the designer clothes, jewelry, and makeup. Her unpolished nails, cracked, dirty, and chewed, testified to her fall from power and wealth. All that was left was the withered and leathered face of Ivanka Trump. The Botox treatments had worn off, replaced by warts and tuffs of hair. Her dirty, ripped, and oversized dress hung loosely around her scrawny body. Like her brothers, she was barefooted and staring into the distance as we approached. When we drew near, she looked toward us without really seeing us.

"Spare some change?" she mumbled.

"Not today, Ivanka," the general replied.

"You know my name," she responded. "How do you know me? Do I know you? I don't recognize you. No one has known my name nor spoken to me by name since I woke up one day in this terrible Hellhole. I need to get back to my businesses and money and clothes and jewelry and servants and cars and mansions and food. Can you help me? Will you get me out of here?"

"No, Ivanka, I cannot help you. This is your place in your own father's Hell. You will never leave here, Ivanka."

She nodded glumly and scratched her head. I saw blood oozing from her scalp. "Lice," Arnold whispered. "She has a bad case of lice."

"Can you tell me where my husband is?" Ivanka asked. "My children? My father and brothers? Why don't they come to visit me? The bastards. Where are they?"

"You will never see your family again," Arnold said. "Hell has no visiting hours. Hell has no visits."

"I am a Jew. I don't believe in Hell."

"What you believe in your head has no bearing on reality. It was always that way, though, wasn't it? You lit candles on Shabbos, but the parts of the Law about mercy and compassion for society's outcasts? Caring for orphans, widows, and sojourners?" Arnold took his hat off for a moment and passed his palm over his head. "So now, you are alone, separated from your dysfunctional family and your so-called society friends. You are condemned to watch these men and women of the Gaza Strip go about their daily lives while you live in constant pain and chronic hunger. You sleep on the streets. You are unnoticed and invisible to the people here.

For all eternity, you *are* the people you belittled and disdained during your lifetime. You are the peasants and children who worked in your sweatshops and sewed your ugly clothing designs. You are nobody's sweetheart. In fact, you are nobody to anybody, period. Including us. Goodbye."

With that, we continued down the street.

Another hundred yards. Maybe more, maybe less. I was disorientated and lost. We turned a corner, crossed an intersection, and slipped into another side alley where we found another old man lying on the ground. He wore a faded and torn pair of pants but was naked from the waist up and, again, barefooted. I did not recognize him but had a guess: "Jared?"

"Yes," said the General. "Good day to you, Mr. Kushner."

At that, the old man stirred and slowly sat up. He looked in our direction, but his eye sockets were hollowed out—empty except for some swollen skin and scar tissue.

"They tore his eyes out when he was assigned here decades ago," Arnold said. "They are still angry at his arrogance, his ego, his pride. Imagine this. A rich, spoiled little brat, the heir of a real estate empire. His father is imprisoned for illegal campaign contributions, tax evasion, and witness tampering, so his son takes over the business. Through a series of incompetent moves, he soon finds himself on the edge of bankruptcy, failure, and foreclosure. In comes his wife Ivanka and father-in-law, who helped him stay on his feet with shady loans and deals involving Russian and Saudi money. When his father-in-law wins the presidency in 2016, he appoints said son-in-law as a senior White House advisor. He puts him in charge of the Israeli-Palestinian conflict, the COVID-19 pandemic, and more.

"Jared brags to the press that he read 25 books on the Israeli-Palestinian conflict so that he could negotiate a peace. So, in truth, reading those books maybe was a good idea. But it in no way made him qualified to be the person in charge of this complex, ongoing concern. And many of the Middle East's policies of Trump's administration made finding a solution to the Israeli-Palestinian conflict ever more remote, at best.

"In addition, he chaired a meeting, in the White House, early in 2020, as the pandemic was spreading. He decided, and this is true and well-documented, against any significant federal action to curb or mitigate the spread of the virus because, wait for it . . . the pandemic was primarily affecting blue states—states that had more Democrats than Republicans.

"He recommended no federal measures to fight the pandemic because he thought it would kill more Democrats than Republicans. We know, of course, that the opposite took place because so many members of Trump's base refused to get vaccinated or wear masks. But in the early stages of the pandemic, it was affecting the blue states the most, so, with Jared's support and recommendation, Trump turned his attention and that of the administration the other way.

"Jared and Ivanka cashed in their connections to their dad to the tune of a total 4-year income of between $172,000,000 and $640,000,000 during his presidency! (Levin, 2021)

"It seems their love of money exceeded even their love of Donald. Seriously, I ask you, how much money does a person need to live a good life? They would not stop looting and pillaging. Indeed, they could not stop. Their greed and their love of money was the root of their identities. So now, they are sentenced to eternity as penniless peasants, outcasts wandering the streets in Gaza, condemned to asking for alms and receiving the same 'no' they gave to those who needed and asked for help from them in life. Their eternal hunger, lice-filled hair and clothing, abscessed teeth, and raw, bare feet stand in contrast to the unfettered consumption they feasted on in life while ignoring the needs of the world's people and those struggling in poverty around the world. They had so much. They were in the right place at the right time to take advantage of the markets, the Trump movement, and their own insider information that, coupled with policy decisions made that benefited them, helped them get out of debt and into the top tier of the world's wealth. But they never blessed anyone else, they never shared their resources."

"Are we finished here?" I asked, cautiously hoping we'd seen enough of the Trump family.

"We have one more visit to make," came Arnold's reply. "Forward."

We continued our walking another quarter mile or so and found another poor old woman, huddled in the corner of a stone wall outside a governmental building. On the way, I had wondered who we might find next, and my guess was correct: Melania.

"Ms. Trump," the General greeted her as we came before her. "How are you?"

"How do I look, you cruel son of a bitch?" she spat back. Truly, she looked terrible. Tear streaks could be seen on her face. Her hair was shorn, face hallowed, eyes swollen, knees and elbows scrapped. She looked away and began rocking, moaning, and muttering. Again, I thought, oh, how the mighty have fallen.

"She can't talk sensibly, I'm afraid," Arnold said. "She lost her mind here, what little of it she had left. She lost part of it when she made the decision to yoke herself to Donald, and more, during his presidency and in the years after he died. Though she always put up that famous face of indifference, she was quite wounded and hurt by the criticism of her husband and, of course, the criticism she brought on herself.

"She was a terrible First Lady, of course—the Anti-Michelle Obama. Though she plagiarized from Michelle, she lacked the grace, intelligence, empathy, and decency of her predecessor.

"There was one thing many Americans did appreciate about her, though, and that was her off-and-on scorn for her husband. The slapping away of his hand, her failure to accompany him on so many of his speaking engagements. The separate bedrooms in the White House.

"But, by and by, Americans and the world learned that she basically shared her husband's worldview. She was a white supremist. She opposed immigration of racial minorities to the U.S. even though she herself was an immigrant. She was, in essence, a porn star, a model who posed naked for money and whose looks attracted Donald Trump. Her jacket with the words on the back, 'I really don't care. Do U?' could not have been any more direct and transparent. She did not give a damn about anyone or anything except herself. And her son Barron.

"Think of what she did. She plagiarized. Her signature First Lady theme was 'Be Best.' To this day, no one, including Melania, knows what that means. She spoke about reducing cyber bullying. Really? You can't make this up. She was married to the worst cyber bully in world history. The best thing you can say about that is that she never had the patience, drive, or determination to do anything more than give it lip service, so it died a merciful death along with the rest of her legacy as First Lady.

"You know, of course, like most of the world who paid attention to these things, that Barron ran away from home on his 18th birthday. He fled to his mother's native nation of Slovenia and joined an orthodox monastery where he took his vows of poverty, chastity, and obedience. He disappeared from the public and was rarely seen outside the walls of the cloister. He saved himself, in life and the afterlife, and that was really a miracle, given his DNA."

"I'll kill those kids," I thought I heard her mutter.

"Ma'am?" I asked.

"I hate everyone one of them. Junior, Eric, Ivanka, Tiffany. And Jarrrrrrred. They stabbed my husband in the back. They stood in his limelight and cast ugly shadows. They refused to fight for him when he needed it the most. I hate them. I'll kill them if I ever get my hands on them." She looked up, her eyes suddenly focused, clear, and pleading. "Help me," she said. "Can you help me find them?"

My words blurted out before I could stop to weigh them. I said, "Not a chance in Hell."

Arnold grinned. "Good one," he said, tracing a tick-mark onto an invisible scoreboard with his finger.

"Can we go now?"

"Yes, that's it for this level. We can move on again. We'll let them continue to rot in hell. Their placement is again just. Forward."

We walked in silence for several minutes, reworking our

way back to the portal of *Trump's Towering Inferno*.

"Wait just a minute. Can we stay here a bit longer?" I was ready to leave the Trumps but torn about leaving Gaza. I once lived in the Middle East. I loved the people I met and they, in turn, seemed to love and care for me. I enjoyed the food and loved hearing the call to prayer echo throughout the city five times per day. It was a special time in my life, and to clear my head of those who had been placed here, I needed to rest and bask in this culture for a few unsullied moments.

"I understand," Arnold said. "Let's sit down for a moment by this mosque. There is something peaceful here that even I can detect."

And so, we lingered until the sun sank into the sea and the men, women, and children of Gaza headed home.

CHAPTER 9

SENATORS IN SHIT

The itsy bitsy senators climbed up the tower spout
Never to imagine the filth that would come out.
But they remain there because they passed the test
The joy of kissing his ass is what they did the best.

I was getting used to the routine. Visit a level of Hell. See unique and somehow fitting punishments meted out to Trump's slew of enablers. Climb the stairs. Repeat. Yet I was also beginning to feel as trapped as they were, a prisoner and victim in *Trump's Towering Inferno* with no escape hatch or plan.

Once again, though, the General anticipated and addressed my disquiet.

"This is, in fact, the final level of *Trump's Towering Inferno*. Like Dante's *Inferno*, there are nine levels. Dante placed Satan beneath the ninth level at the very pit of Hell itself, although Satan's upper torso and head were visible in the ninth level. This *Inferno* has nine floors, with Trump himself confined to the penthouse just above the ninth level. Once we complete this level, we have only one final stop at the penthouse, and you will be on your way. I know this has been difficult, but it is important for you to see and observe everything so that you can share it with others. That is your role here.

"Unlike those imprisoned here, you are free. You are free to go at any time. No one will prevent you from departing. You have held up well and have only these final visits, and you will then have seen all there is to see. You can go now or stay here a bit longer."

My body responded to these words, like a marathoner pushing for the finish line at mile 25. I nodded. Forward.

The sign on the stairway door affirmed what Arnold had said: I saw the number "9" over the general's shoulder as he reached for the doorknob. "All right?"

"Yes," I replied, "I'm ready." My voice was weak and shaky, but no more so than my body and knees. The surge in energy was more a trickle.

"Forward." The general pulled the door open into the stairwell. As the door opened and I got my first glimpse into this level, we were also greeted with an overwhelming odor. Sewage, I thought. Raw sewage. A septic system?

"It is worse than that," Arnold said. We walked ahead. It was dark. I could not see much. "Let's stand here a moment. Let your eyes adjust."

Two or three minutes passed. It was still too dark for me to see clearly, but the repulsive smell was making me nauseous.

"I forget from time to time that you are human. The smell is overwhelming, and it is too dark for you to see much, if anything. I'll walk you around the room and describe what you might see in the shadows, and we'll return to the staircase for our final flight of stairs. Agreed?"

"Agreed."

He took me by the elbow, and we began walking along the wall to our right.

We took a few slow steps. The floor was smooth and level, and I was beginning to see some shapes in the middle of the room, although it was still too dark to make out anything clearly. The smell was overpowering and disgusting. And getting worse.

"In Dante's *Inferno*, the lower he and Virgil descended, the worst the sins and corresponding punishment in that level. As they descended deeper into Hell, they moved closer and closer to Satan and found men and women who had committed crimes and sins worse than those sentenced at the higher levels, or circles. Here, as we have ascended, we have climbed closer and closer to Trump himself and observed men and women more and more reprehensible and responsible for allowing Trump to become the most powerful man on the planet. Some of the scum lower down were as bad, and sometimes worse, than the men and women placed at higher levels. But here they are grouped together in categories to maintain a sense of order and symmetry. You have seen this on each of the previous levels.

"This ninth level is an exclusive level. These men, and yes, they are all men here, were members of the U.S. Senate during the presidential term of Donald Trump. Do you know the word 'senate' derives from the Latin word *senex*, which means 'old man?' The U.S. Senate was created and designed to be an assembly for esteemed white men (later amended to include women and persons of color) to gather and discuss the most important issues of the day and find common ground in service to their nation. It was President James Buchanan who once quipped that the Senate is the 'world's greatest deliberative body' (Kiely, 2020). Of course, anyone who watches C-Span knows that is not true."

"You watch C-Span," I asked?

"I have access to it, yes. But I don't waste my time watching it. When I see it on the telly from time to time, I see what everyone sees—one or two members sitting in the chamber half-asleep with another member yacking away. They don't speak to each other. They don't try to create consensus, bi-partisan support, or offer compromises. What they do is pander to their bases and jabber for soundbites that can be used at for their next fundraiser.

"Currently, the Senate is a toxic, bitterly divided legislative body split along party lines. Gone are the days of progressive Republicans or traditional Democrats. You won't find Republicans voting for Democratic proposals or legislation, or Democrats supporting a Republican idea. Once upon a time, there were great friendships between individuals from different political parties who did what was best for the people and nation. No more! Now they do what is best for themselves. It is a chamber of self-interests and narcissism."

"So, what's going on here?"

"Well, maybe it is just as well that you can't see much.

"Donald Trump is directly above us in his penthouse. Of course, you know what the word 'penthouse' meant in old English, don't you?"

"No, I can't say that I do."

The general looked sternly at me for a moment, then smiled.

"A 'penthouse' was not originally used to describe a luxury room or apartment at the top of a building, but as an out-building, like a shelter built onto the side of the building with a sloping roof. In the Middle Ages, the clergy used the term *penthouse* for the stable in which Jesus was born. But most often, 'penthouse' meant 'outhouse.' Yes, a place to do your business. Donald Trump is sitting right now in his penthouse outhouse right over our heads.

"Further, he is sitting on his throne. A wooden, one seat toilet that opens to this floor."

I was beginning to put things together. It was not a pretty picture.

"The foul smell you are experiencing," he continued, "is, ahh, how to word this mildly? It's from the excrement emanating from Donald Trump's bowels as gravity pulls it down to this level.

"His bare ass is visible to those who can see. At least, it should be visible. It is protruding into this space like Satan's upper torso in Dante's *Inferno*. It is found in the center of this room."

My feet stopped walking. I froze in place.

"Best to keep walking," the general suggested, while encouraging me forward by taking my elbow in his hand. I acknowledged with a slight nod of my head and began moving forward again, although how I could not say.

"We would see his bare ass right now with a flashlight except there are persons in the way blocking the view. They are getting a close-hand view of how human bodies shed solid waste.

"To a person, the U.S. Senators who supported Donald Trump during and after his term in the White House despised him. Use whatever word or words you prefer: they reviled, loathed, scorned, detested, and hated him. We know this because this is what they told each other, their families, and members of the press in private, off-the-record conversations. As you know, and anyone who ever watched him on TV knows, or met him in person knew, he was the walking incarnation of the seven deadly sins, a caricature of immorality, easily mocked and scorned. He had no friends in his life, only sycophants who rode him on the way to the top. He threw these persons under the bus anytime he needed to. They, in turn, left him the minute it became politically feasible to do so. He was an arsehole's arse.

"Captured here for eternity are the worst butt kissers of all time, four of Trump's Senate flatterers or minions, those who did his bidding, who kissed his arse, who were brown nosers par excellence."

He turned me toward the center of the room.

"Right in front of you are Mitch McConnell, Lindsay Graham, Ted Cruz, and Josh Hawley. They are standing up with lips planted on Trump's arse while he defecates on them for eternity."

"Are you shitting me?"

Arnold grinned and tallied another point on the invisible scoreboard. "Putting aside your colorful metaphor, no, I am not shitting you. But Donald Trump is shitting on them. And urinating. Right now. Has been since each of them died and was sentenced here. As you know, Hawley just arrived here yesterday. He was processed quickly and sent up. We saw him in the lobby. His place at the arse has been reserved for many years. Mitch, Lindsay, and Ted have company now, and they'll think that's great until they realize that what splatters on Hawley will ricochet directly onto them.

"To make things worse, of course, they all hated each other, too. So now, cheek to cheek and lips to The Donald's arse cheeks, they will spend eternity next to each other while on the receiving end of Trump's business. Ha! 'Cheek to cheek!' I daresay your wit is rubbing off on me!"

"Great" I said. "Can we go now?"

Josh Hawley

Arnold picked up the pace. Within a few quick strides, we were back at the door to the staircase. I stepped through the doorway and slumped down on the first step.

"I can't take much more of this," I sighed.

"You won't have to. One final stop. Take a moment, then we'll proceed.

"Thanks." It was all I could say.

CHAPTER 10

DONALD TRUMP: "YOU'RE FIRED!"

Twinkle twinkle Donald Trump
No more phonies to kiss your rump.
As you quickly descended to Hell
It was no surprise how far you fell.

I was falling. Free falling, spread eagled, face down, like a cat dropping from a height. The fall was in slow motion—falling, but not as fast as gravity would have it. I was outside the tower, but I could see through the walls. I was seeing the different floors of *Trump's Towering Inferno*.

Yes, I went past the senators puckering up in the darkness, then Trump's family members placed in Gaza. Next, I saw the advisors and representatives, followed by the press secretaries and governors. Then the "clergy," the news anchors, and, at the base, or first floor, the foundation from which Trump arose.

But I kept falling. There was a subway vent, and it was open. I plunged right through and found myself approaching an underground cavern. It spiraled down deep into the earth. I could see concentric layers, with people on each level, twisting and turning in agony. I knew immediately it was Dante's *Inferno*. Here I passed the first circle, those in limbo including Homer, Socrates, and Plato. Below it I saw those guilty of lust, and the next lower level was reserved for gluttons. I kept dropping and descended past the levels of avarice and prodigality, then wrath and sullenness. Then, those guilty of heresy, followed by the violent. The eighth level was filled with those who had committed fraud, through seduction, flattery, sorcerers, and false prophets. This was the level for liars and thieves.

I saw the final level, the circle reserved for treachery. A frozen lake lay at the bottom of this level. I could make out Satan, held in the ice. His three heads were filled with victims. Although I could not identify them, I knew who they were: Brutus, Cassius, and Judas. I was headed directly toward Satan when . . .

I heard a voice. Faint, at first, then growing louder. "Professor. Professor Lavender."

I opened my eyes. There was General Arnold, with a cool cloth whipping my forehead.

"Wha . . . what just happened?" I asked.

"You fainted mate. You were out cold for a few minutes. One minute you were sitting on the stairs, and the next falling forward. I grabbed your shoulders and pulled you back onto the landing."

Suddenly I remembered where we had been. Arnold lifted a corner of his coat. "Water," he asked. He offered me his canteen and I took a long slug. I felt a bit better.

I struggled back to a sitting position and rubbed my eyes.

"We're almost done," said the general. "Are you strong enough to finish?"

Was I? Could I really proceed to the top of the *Towering Inferno?* What a question. I was certainly *not* ready to proceed but believed in my heart that I needed to move forward. Yes, I had a choice, but having come this far, why not finish? And, the truth is, I was interested, curious what I would see at the final stop. It was forward up that staircase, or an eternity of regret.

"I'm as ready now as I ever will be," I said.

"Up we go." He was strangely upbeat.

He helped me to my feet. We turned and began climbing the stairs. The stairway narrowed so that just one person at a time could climb. I fell in step behind the General. The steps led to a small landing with a familiar-looking door, but instead of the expected number 10 on it, I read instead "Roof."

"There's no 10th floor?" I asked.

"No. You'll see."

He opened the door. Fresh, cool air filled the stairwell and my lungs. Ahhhhhh! How long had it been since I breathed fresh air, I wondered? We stepped into the night on top of this building in the middle of Manhattan. It was a clear, dark night. As usual, there were few stars to be seen above the city lights. Was it early? Late? Just before dawn? I had no sense of time, but, still, it was nice to be outside again.

Fifty steps or so in front of us was a simple wooden structure. It was no more than five feet long by five feet wide, with a sloping roof starting at a height of maybe eight feet dropping down to seven. It had a crescent moon on the side.

"This is Trump's Penthouse. This is where the ex-president will spend eternity. This is his *Inferno*."

There was a line of people stretching across the roof and arching down from the sky. They were on what appeared to be an invisible stairway. The line seemed endless.

There was a second invisible stairway leading back up into the Heavens. I could make out a few individuals, spread out, climbing those steps before fading from sight.

The man at the front of the line opened the door to Trump's penthouse. I saw him engage in a conversation with Trump, then slammed the door shut. Bright red and orange lights shone through the crescent shaped opening. The lights flickered for a few minutes before fading. The person who had opened and closed the door moved off to the left and toward the ascending stairway. The next person in line moved forward. I could not discern what was happening.

"Want a closer look?"

I *was* curious. "Yes."

We walked toward the shed and long queue of persons in line.

"Let's watch from here," the general said, positioning me a few feet from the door on the side with the crescent moon.

The person now first in line opened the door. I could see a naked Donald Trump sitting on a wooden seat. This was not a pretty sight! He was obviously inside an outhouse sitting over a hole. I knew now that the senators were there below.

"Why is he naked?" I asked.

"Don't you see? It's another metaphor. The president had no clothes on, just like the famous emperor. Everyone knew it. He had no governing principles, no core beliefs. He had no political agenda, no conservative or Republican philosophy or doctrines to stand by. Donald Trump's first and only principle was to do what was best for Donald Trump. He did not defend the Constitution of the United States. He did not defend the people of the United States. He did not serve members of his family, his party, or his base. Donald Trump was all about Donald Trump. He was famously transparent on this, and everyone knew it. The emperor, er, the president, had no clothes on."

While Arnold was speaking with me, the man at the front of the line leaned forward and asked Donald a simple question: "Did you win the presidential election of 2020?"

Trump turned shades of red and purple.

"Watch this," Arnold quipped, nudging me a step closer.

"No. I lost. I came close to winning in the Electoral College but lost the popular vote by over seven million votes," I heard Trump say. He continued:

"I created 'The Big Lie' to save face and to position myself for another run at the presidency in 2024. My family, attorneys and inner circle knew this, but they wanted me to have a second term as much as I did because of the power and privilege it gave them, so they got in line and echoed and spread this fake news. It continued to spread and had life for years, even after I died."

"Trump has been given an extra level of punishment here," Arnold said. "Like the conniving attorney Fletcher Reede (played by Jim Carrey) in *Liar Liar*, Donald is compelled to tell only the truth from now into eternity. You can see it pains him to do so. No matter what the question, he must be honest. He must answer each question truthfully, like you just witnessed. Now, watch what happens next."

The person at the front of the line said these words, with emphasis: "For this and many other reasons, you are fired!"

He then slammed the door shut in Trump's face.

I heard a loud roar. Flames filled the penthouse and flickered out the small openings. Muffled screams escaped through the doorway. A whisp of smoke emerged from a small pipe on the roof of the penthouse I had not previously seen.

"The interior walls of the penthouse are identical to the walls of a crematorium. After telling the truth to whatever question he is asked, Trump is fired by the individual who asked him the question, and then burned alive, physically 'fired,' trapped in his penthouse, in Hell.

"What is happening right now is that Donald Trump is burning in Hell, right behind that closed door. He will burn for a few minutes before succumbing. It's a terrible death, being burned alive. And, you see, there is no stop, drop and roll in hell. He burns up, over and over again."

As Trump burned, the person at the front of the line moved off and began climbing the unseen stairway to Heaven. The next in line took his place and waited for the flames to fade.

"Like the mythological phoenix that rises from the ashes, Trump's roasting takes place repeatedly. He comes back to life, faces a new question, tells the truth, against his will, I might say, and is summarily fired by the voter who has just asked him a question. He is then physically fired, cremated alive, by the flames inside his penthouse. This will go on for eternity. It is his punishment and destiny."

"Voter? You said voter?"

"Yes, the line you see stretching down from the Heavens are the 81,268,924 persons who voted for Joseph Biden to be the president of the United States in 2020. In fact, they, too, are avatars, as the 81-plus million have better things to do. But these are the persons who literally fired Donald Trump in 2020 and fire him, literally, every day now and into eternity."

A few minutes passed. Trump had "come back" to life and resumed his position defecating on the senators below. A woman, next in line, opened the door to the penthouse and asked this:

"Did you really trust Putin more than the CIA and other U.S. spy agencies?"

Again. Anger. Red face. Squirming.

"No, of course not. I knew Putin was lying. He and his Russian colleagues and spy agencies clearly interfered in the 2016 election and helped me win that election. But if I admitted that the Russians helped me win, that would have cast a shadow over my presidency and made me look weak. So, I had to trash the CIA and American agencies to show my strength."

The woman slammed the door shut while saying these words: "For this and many other reasons, you are fired!"

Redux. Roar of fire. Flames at the window. Smoke escaping.

I estimated that from the time each new question was asked until the cycle ran its course and a new voter emerged with another question was a period of maybe 15 minutes. Another individual came forward:

"Were you more interested in your own business and profits than the best interests of the United States?"

Repeat. Anger. Red face. Squirming.

"I was a businessman, first and foremost. I put my profits ahead of anything and everyone else. That's why I outsourced most of my businesses to China, because the labor there was dirt cheap, and I could make larger profits. 'Make America Great Again,' MAGA, really meant Make Donald More Affluent. Of course, I put my bottom line and interests ahead of the United States. Duh!"

The door was slammed shut again. "For this and many other reasons, you are fired!"

Again. Roar of fire. Flames at the window. Smoke escaping.

I took the time between the voter's questions, Trump's truthful answers and his subsequent firing and restoration to look at the General.

"Wow," I said.

"Wow indeed. It was the presidential historian Michael Beschloss who once said in an interview, 'I have never seen a president in American history who has lied so continuously and so outrageously as Donald Trump, period' (Timm 2020). Beschloss was, of course, speaking the truth. Lying to the American public was bad. But his traitorous behavior was far worse. He is not burning in Hell because of his lies. He is burning in Hell because he was, and take it from me as one who knows, the worst traitor to the United States ever. Worse than me, Benedict Arnold."

Another voted stepped forward: "Did you lie about the COVID-19 pandemic," she asked?

Once more. Anger. Red face. Squirming.

"Of course, I lied about COVID-19. I was briefed early in the pandemic and understood how bad it was going to be. The recordings Bob [Woodward] took of our conversations made it perfectly clear how much I knew and when I knew it.

"But I wanted to be re-elected. I blamed China—that's why I used the phrase 'Kung-Flu.' Its why I refused to wear a mask in public, and why I hid how sick I was when I caught the virus during the 2020 campaign."

"For this and many other reasons, you are fired!"

The door was slammed shut. At this distance, I could not only hear the roar of the flames but could feel the heat. The flames flickered again through the window: the smoke rose. The screams were heard. The voter moved off toward the ascending stairway, and another took her place. A few minutes later:

"Did it rain during your inauguration speech at the U.S. Capitol? You said it did not rain until the event was over."

Again. Anger. Red face. Squirming.

"Of course, it rained. It rained through my speech and most of the ceremony. Anyone who was there in person or watching on the television could see that."

Redux. The roar of the fire. The red of the flames dancing through the window, smoke rising from the pipe.

"Who drew the little sharpie mark on the map of the Southeastern U.S. as Hurricane Dorian approached the coast on September 4, 2019," asked the next Biden voter in line.

"I did. I had tweeted that Alabama was in danger, when the national hurricane office had issued no warning for Alabama. I made a mistake but could not admit that. So, I took a sharpie pen and made my own cone of warning. My staff pressured federal experts to say I was correct, and that they were wrong, but to no avail. I was the president and had the power behind me, so why not use it?"

"For this and many other reasons, you are fired!"

She then slammed the door shut in Trump's face. Roar of fire. Flames at the window. Smoke escaping.

Next up, a young man in jeans, a tee-shirt, and Birkenstocks.

"You claimed on the campaign trail that Joe Biden, if elected, was going to end the protection Americans enjoyed as the result of the Affordable Care Act, which had been passed during the Obama-Biden Administration, and which you tried to weaken but which Biden promised to uphold. Did you think Biden was going to destroy these protections?"

Ask. Watch. Burn. Repeat.

Next up. An elderly woman. Question: "Were you unable to release your financial statements and taxes because you were under audit?"

Anger. Red face. Squirming.

"We were under audit. I had so many businesses, and it seemed like one or more was always under audit. The audits took so long, I think, because we worked so hard to hide information from the auditors. But this was an excuse. There is no law against releasing financials while under audit. I did not want the American public to see what a fraud I was, and where I had cheated the government and my business associates. So, I refused to release them. I claimed I could not release them because of ongoing audits, but that was not true. Once my taxes were released after my death, it was clear what I was hiding."

"For this and many other reasons, you are fired!"

Door slam. Roar. Fire at the window. Smoke snaking towards the sky.

Another pause as Trump burns, followed a few moments later by another voter:

"Did you and your dad commit crimes against persons of color in your apartment sales?"

You get the picture. Although he did not want to do it, he was forced to tell the truth, over and over, for eternity.

"Yes. We did not want black or brown people living in our housing projects. Not in Manhattan, not in Queens, not anywhere."

"For this and many other reasons, you are fired!"

"Did you cheat at golf?"

"Did you shit in your pants?"

"Did you sleep with Stormy Daniels shortly after your son Barron was born, and then pay her to buy her silence?"

"Did you have fantasies of sleeping with Ivanka?"

We watched this for a few hours. It was painfully satisfying. The Great Traitor and Liar in Chief coming clean by debunking his lies. And then being punished. The Greatest Traitor in the history of the United States. Burning in Hell. Over and over again.

"You have seen enough. Are you ready to go?"

"Absolutely." I thought we would never get to this. Now that the time had arrived, I could not get away from here quickly enough.

But I did have one last question. Arnold looked at me and, nodding his head, said, "Go ahead and ask."

"Well, on the ninth level, just below us, we saw, well, you saw and described to me, four senators who were kissing The Donald's derriere and getting his business up close and personal. What happens to them when Trump is burning?"

"Well, their lips burn, of course. Trump burns into ashes while their lips are still locked in place. Their lips burn, swell, blister, and bleed. They get a quick reprieve while the process of his return to life takes place but are then again locked into position. Trump's shit becomes a kind of lip balm, a lip shit stick if you will. It's not pretty."

I was sorry I asked.

I looked around and saw dawn and a faint light emerging towards the east as the sun was about to usher in a new day. I was beginning to see the city's skyline. We walked toward the southern side of the building.

A few Capitol Hill police offers appeared. Had they been there all along? I could not say. I had not seen them until just now. They greeted me and took me by the arms right up to the edge. I looked down—I've always felt uncomfortable with heights, but more at ease now. I trusted these police officers.

They strapped me into a harness. My mind was swimming from all I had witnessed since walking through the doors to Trump Tower. The general stepped forward and said: "It's been longer than a day, Dr. Lavender. Today is Sunday, April 4. Easter morning. You have been inside for almost 48 hours. Hear the church bells beginning to peal in the city. Happy Easter, my friend."

"Easter greetings to you as well, my friend."

The harness was in place. I was hooked to a wire, and an officer spoke gently these words: "You are on a zip line now that will take you down to the front steps of St. Patrick's Cathedral. You will be met by more Capitol Hill police officers, who will help you out of your harness. You will then be on your way."

I looked at the General. "See you below," he said.

And, with that, I was off, my first zip lining experience and it took place in the heart of New York City, from the top of *Trump's Towering Inferno* down to New York's most famous church. I could not suppress the smile on my face for the enjoyable ride.

As I approached the cathedral, I slowed down. Two officers "caught" me and steadied me on my feet. A moment later, the harness was off and so were they. I was standing again next to General Arnold.

"Here are some refreshments. You should partake."

I saw a platter of food. There were dates, homemade flour tortillas and challah bread in front of fresh fruit and vegetables. I also saw glasses filled with fruit drinks. I took a few dates in hand and put one in my mouth. It was soft, sweet, and delicious. Some juice to wash it down. It was Heavenly.

"What's next?"

"You can leave whenever you are ready," he said. "There is your wife in your car. She is ready to drive you back home to Connecticut. With a divine gift, the trip will take place the moment you get into the passenger seat. You will be home when you get in the car."

I looked and, sure enough, there sat Maureen in our metallic gray Impreza.

"And what about you, General? What's next for you?"

"Forward. A general always scans the horizon for what's next. I will go forward."

I wanted to know more but knew that was not likely. He thrust his hand before me, and we shook hands. He said simply, "Godspeed, Dr. Lavender. It has been a privilege."

And, with that, he turned and melted into the crowd, as you could at no other place on the planet but New York City, where no one noticed a middle-aged man wearing a 200+-year-old, faded American Revolutionary War officer's uniform walking down the streets of Manhattan.

DANTE REDUX, REDUX, REDUX

We have come to the end of our journey. At least, the end of *Dante Redux*.

I read somewhere that Bruce Springsteen and the E Street Band spent six months working on the song *Born to Run*, and 14 months working on the album of the same name. Bruce obsessed over every syllable and note, and re-wrote, re-worked, re-hashed, re-played and re-recorded every song time and time again. The night before he and the band were scheduled to begin a road trip with live performances from the album, Springsteen was still not satisfied, wanted to delay the tour and keep working on it. His manager reportedly said: "Bruce, *Born to Run* is finished. Anything else you have will go on your next album." Or something to that effect. The album was finished and released. It is one of the greatest rock 'n roll albums of all time.

Last night my wife said to me, "Wayne, *Dante Redux* is finished. Anything else you have will go into your next book." Or something to that effect.

But the story of the Donald Trump Personality Cult is not finished. It seems that every day there are new revelations about . . . his business, his taxes, his personal life, his campaign for the presidency in 2016, his presidency, his post-2020 election and actions on 1.6.2021, his post-presidency. The world according to Trump has not come to an end.

And, so, there will be a need for *Dante Redux Redux*. Oh my!

I'm not an artist. I have no talent for drawing, painting, or sculpture. I can't sing or play an instrument. I cannot act or perform on stage, a movie or TV set. I am not a poet and recognize the limits of my writing talent.

But I do know right from wrong. The path Donald Trump is taking and leading his followers down is going in the wrong direction. Full stop.

We are clearly at an inflection, or tipping point, in the great American Experiment. Of course, there have been other times of challenge we have faced as Americans. When George Washington was preparing to cross the Delaware River on the cold, snowy night of December 25, 1776, the fate of his army and the fledging idea of independence and the new nation were still up in the air, as it was when the British invaded and burned down federal building in Washington, D.C., in 1814. The nation stood on the brink as Abraham Lincoln wrote and delivered this memorable sentence at the close of his first inauguration on the eve of the American Civil War: "The mystic chords of memory, stretching from every battlefield and patriot grave to every living heart and hearthstone all over this broad land, will yet swell the chorus of the Union, when again touched, as surely they will be, by the better angels of our nature."

We survived the Civil War and assassination of Abraham Lincoln. We came through World War I and the Great Depression. When Pearl Harbor was attacked on December 7, 1941, it was Franklin Delano Roosevelt who rallied the nation declaring it as "a date which will live in infamy." America survived through the assassinations of John Kennedy, Malcom X, Martin Luther King, Jr., and Bobby Kennedy. We endured the civil rights riots in the 1960s, Viet Nam and the terrorist attacks of September 11, 2001. We are still here. And we will be here. But the nature of our democracy and national identity is uncertain.

The great difference between these historic moments and our contemporary situation is the level of bald-faced lying and hypocrisy now stemming from Trump, his cronies, and most of the Republican Party to which he controls. We have now, because of gerrymandering, voter suppression, and the flawed electoral college, a minority-controlled nation. Republican leaders, elected and appointed, are doing their best to turn the clock back to what they see as the golden time in U.S. history when people of color were kept "in their places" and white Americans held all the positions of power in the political and business communities.

To be clear, there is no current Republican platform or agenda for moving the United States forward on the world stage. They have no healthcare policies, approaches to global climate change, infrastructure maintenance or immigration policies. They don't address prison reform, the COVID-19 pandemic and endemic phase of this disease, the rising rates of crime and inflation, reasonable gun control, world water or food policies. They have no plans to help persons out of poverty or to improve education in the U.S., or any other policy issues.

Instead, we hear a constant stream of personal attacks on Democrats that have nothing to do with the polices they are proposing. They turn to the culture war and create and exploit divisive issues like Critical Race Theory—whatever that actually is—asylum-seeking Central American migrants hoping to cross the southern border of the U.S., the LGBT communities, White Replacement Theory and The Big Lie of the "stolen" election.

We know that most Republican leaders and elected officials know the difference between right and wrong. We know this because we have them on video and audio tape speaking the truth about Trump, his presidency, his loss in the 2020 election and his role in the violent insurrection on January 6. In these video and audio tapes they are highly critical of Trump (Martin and Burns, 2022). But when confronted by members of the press, they dismiss, deny, or ignore the words they have spoken or claim that their words were taken out of context by the fake press that is attempting to silence them. They must think the electorate is either stupid or does not care. Maybe both. We remember Trump's speech in 2016 when he said, "I love the poorly educated!" (Stevenson, 2016).

These Republican leaders have no shame. Their love for and obsession with power exceeds their devotion to our nation, the U.S. Constitution, and their constituency.

Inferno was the inspiration for this book. Artists, like Dante, create stories that help form our worldview through their work, be it music, paintings, theater, movie, or literature. Great artists address the eternally contemporary questions of human existence, such as: Why am I here? Is there an afterlife? Does God exist? What is love? Justice? Truth? And, maybe the most important question of all, what is the meaning of life?

I have done my best to channel Dante's spirit and create a parallel tome for a different time and place. I sit next to Rodin as he creates *The Thinker* to portray Dante looking down on the Hell he created, and with Spencer Tracy as he brought Dante's *Inferno* to the big screen in 1935. It seems that human nature is the same, and the allure of fame, power, and riches still calls. Those described in this book have clearly fallen to these temptations and pushed the tiller of the ship of state toward the rocks. Being a public servant is not supposed to be defined by selfishness and immorality. Hence, "servant." The United States, like every other nation, has a long history of men and women who sacrificed for this nation, who asked not what the nation could do for them but what they could do for their nation. I personally know many elected and appointed officials who seek nothing else than to serve the public's best interests. Theirs is a noble calling.

People of good conscience debate public policy, as they do sports, religion, and every other topic. It is okay for Republicans and Democrats to have different agendas and different solutions to the issues of our days: working through these issues for the best interests of the American public should be the goal. Instead, we are living in a time where what is good for the nation takes a seat behind Republican leaders who are doing what is best for the Republican Party and themselves.

I do feel a degree of remorse for creating this work of fiction. But I am also aware of a sense of justice. I may not believe in a literal Hell, nor a God who would punish his or her children by condemning them to Hell, but it sure feels good to call out these individuals and offer an alternative eternal reality to them for their association with Trump and the damage he left behind.

The Donald's motive for power was greed, as was his drive for attention. He was subject to an insatiable need for both power and possession that neither his acquisitions nor position as the president of the United States could satisfy. The more power he got, the more power he sought; likewise, the more wealth he obtained, the more he craved. (Hamilton 1930:142) He is a terribly sick man, as most Americans and citizens of the world know, cut from the same cloth as other despots.

In other circumstances, I could feel compassion for Trump. One would be forgiven for feeling pity for this man-child. It is possible to hold anger and empathy together. But the damage he has created, and continues to create, far exceeds my sympathy. Thus, *Trump's Towering Inferno*.

That said, I am a firm believer in repentance coupled with forgiveness.

I am not anticipating or expecting this, but if any of the men and women so written about in this work ever see that there is a sliver of truth found herein, they can still redeem themselves by walking back their connections to this venal individual and publicly proclaiming what they say in private every day: that, indeed, the 45th president of the United States had no moral clothes on. He stood naked on the world's stage, an amoral, decadent individual who was concerned solely about his own interests. To be sure, sometimes the interests of the United States and the world paralleled his personal concerns. At times, 45 even made decisions that served the people of the United States. As the saying goes, even a blind squirrel finds an acorn now and then. But, overall, Trump was a repeat traitor to the oath of office he took on January 20, 2017. This book is a warning to those who want to continue down this path: let those who have eyes see.

—Wayne Lavender
July 4, 2022

REFERENCES

Brown, Robert McAfee. 1985. *The Bible Speaks to You*. Philadelphia: Westminster Press.

Conscientia, Liberatatis, and Centesimus Annus. 2019. "5 Things to Know about the Preferential Option for the Poor." *Saint John Institute*. Retrieved May 12, 2022 (https://www.saintjohninstitute.org/five-things-to-know-about-the-preferential-option-for-the-poor/).

Cox, Harvey Gallagher. 1965. *God's Revolution and Man's Responsibility*. Valley Forge: Judson Press.

Elliot, Phili, and Zeke Miller. 2016. "Inside Donald Trump's Chaotic Transition." *Time* (November 18, 2016).

Esper, Mark T. 2022. *A Sacred Oath: Memoirs of a Secretary of Defense During Extraordinary Times*. William Morrow.

Falwell, Jerry. 2004. "God Is Pro-War." *Listen America*. Retrieved September 12, 2011 (http://www.wnd.com/news/article.asp?ARTICLE_ID=36859).

First Baptist Dallas. 2019. *Dr. Robert Jeffress on Pelosi Calling for Prayer over Dems Pursuit to Impeachment President*.

Fox News. 2019. *Pastor Jeffress Talks Evangelical Reaction to Stormy Daniels*.

Guthrie, Woodie. 1954. "Old Man Trump." Retrieved August 2, 2021 (https://woodyguthrie.org/Lyrics/Old_Man_Trump.htm).

Hamilton, Alexander, James Madison, and John Jay. 1982. *The Federalist Papers*. New York, N.Y.: Bantam Books.

Hamilton, Edith. 1930. *The Greek Way*. New York: W. W. Norton & company, inc.

Kessler, Glenn, Salvador Rizzo, and Meg Kelly. 2021. "Analysis | Trump's False or Misleading Claims Total 30,573 over 4 Years." *Washington Post*.

Kiely, Kathy. 2020. "Five Myths about the U.S. Senate: No, It Is Not the World's 'Greatest Deliberative Body'— and It's Not Stuck in the Past." *The Washington Post (Online)*. Retrieved September 19, 2021 (http://www.proquest.com/usmajordailies/docview/2349100749/citation/74B5F2B5F3C54027PQ/5).

Kranish, Michael. 2021. "The Making of Madison Cawthorn: How Falsehoods Helped Propel the Career of a New pro-Trump Star of the Far Right." *The Washington Post (Online)*. Retrieved August 31, 2021 (http://www.proquest.com/usmajordailies/docview/2493888910/citation/8669CB66311D4D04PQ/1).

Lemon, Jason. 2019. "Trump Spiritual Adviser Paula White Prays against President's Opponents, Suggests They 'Operate in Sorcery and Witchcraft.'" *Newsweek*. Retrieved August 10, 2021 (https://www.newsweek.com/trump-spiritual-adviser-paula-white-prays-against-presidents-opponents-suggests-they-operate-1470197).

Levin, Bess. 2021. "Jared and Ivanka Made Up to $640 Million While Working in Washington, or 457,142 Stimulus Checks." *Vanity Fair Blogs*. Retrieved September 18, 2021 (https://www.vanityfair.com/news/2021/02/jared-kushner-ivanka-trump-white-house-income).

Lind, Dara. 2017. "Trump's White House Called Its First Press Briefing to Complain about Reporters' Tweets." *Vox*.

Retrieved August 25, 2021 (https://www.vox.com/2017/1/21/14347812/trump-press-briefing-sean-spicer).

March, Mary Tyler. 2019. "Trump Ramps up Rhetoric on Media, Calls Press 'the Enemy of the People.'" *TheHill*. Retrieved August 21, 2021 (https://thehill.com/homenews/administration/437610-trump-calls-press-the-enemy-of-the-people).

Martin, James Kirby. 1997. *Benedict Arnold, Revolutionary Hero: An American Warrior Reconsidered*. New York: New York University Press.

Martin, Jonathan, and Alexander Burns. 2022. *This Will Not Pass: Trump, Biden, and the Battle for America's Future*. New York: Simon & Schuster.

Meacham, Jon. 2018. *The Soul of America: The Battle for Our Better Angels*. Random House Publishing Group.

NowThis News. 2019. *Trump's Faith Advisor Paula White Is Now a White House Staffer | NowThis*.

NRSV, Bible. 1991. *The New Oxford Annotated Bible*. Oxford, Toronto, New York: Oxford University Press, Inc.

Peck, M. Scott. 1983. *People of the Lie: The Hope for Healing Human Evil*. New York: Simon and Schuster.

Posner, Sarah. 2020. *Unholy : Why White Evangelicals Worship at the Altar of Donald Trump /*. New York: Random House.

Shear, Michael. 2020. "Inside the Failure: 5 Takeaways on Trump's Effort to Shift Responsibility - The New York Times." Retrieved September 12, 2021 (https://web.archive.org/web/20200719135216/https://www.nytimes.

com/2020/07/18/us/politics/trump-coronavirus-failure-takeaways.html?campaign_id=9&emc=edit_nn_2020 0719&instance_id=20443&nl=the-morning&regi_id= 65333603&segment_id=33788&te=1&user_id=3f9f326f 3fbb4cdd48c16dc0088afe81).

Sokolsky, Aaron David Miller, Richard. 2019. "Pompeo Might Go down as the Worst Secretary of State in Modern Times." *CNN*. Retrieved May 20, 2022 (https://www.cnn.com/2019/10/05/opinions/mike-pompeo-worst-secre tary-of-state-miller-sokolsky/index.html).

Solzhenitsyn, Alexander. 1973. *The Gulag Archipelago, 1918-1956*. London: Collins/Fontana.

Stevenson, Peter. 2016. "Donald Trump Loves the 'Poorly Educated'—and Just about Everyone Else in Nevada." *Washington Post*, February 24.

Timm, Jane. 2020. "Trump versus the Truth: The Most Outrageous Falsehoods of His Presidency." *NBC News*. Retrieved October 14, 2021 (https://www.nbcnews.com/politics/donald-trump/trump-versus-truth-most-outrag eous-falsehoods-his-presidency-n1252580).

Toobin, Jeffrey. 2008. "The Dirty Trickster." *The New Yorker*, May 23.

Unger, Harlow. 2002. *Lafayette*. New York: John Wiley and Sons.

Wang, Amy. 2021. "Birx Tells CNN Most U.S. Covid Deaths 'Could Have Been Mitigated' after First 100,000." *Washington Post*, March 27.

ABOUT THE AUTHOR

Wayne Lavender is a United Methodist pastor, an author, speaker, and educator now serving as the executive director of the Foundation 4 Orphans and professor at Quinnipiac University. In addition to leading four congregations as a pastor, he has taught at the University of Human Development in Sulaymaniyah, Iraq, Virginia Wesleyan, and George Mason Universities. He is an author of seven previous books as well as numerous published articles and essays. He lives close to nature with his wife Maureen in Hamden, Connecticut.

ABOUT THE ILLUSTRATOR

Don Landgren Jr. has been drawing award-winning editorial cartoons for 40 years. His cartoons appear in the Worcester Telegram & Gazette as well as in USAToday and many other Gannett newspapers. His work has won 99 awards from many newspaper associations for his editorial cartoons, illustrations, page designs and graphics. He is a member of the Association of American Editorial Cartoonists, the International Society of Caricaturists Artists, and the National Cartoonists Society. He is also a professional caricaturist, drawing for private and corporate events as PARTOONS: Caricatures by Don Landgren Jr.

Related Titles from Westphalia Press

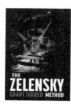

The Zelensky Method
by Grant Farred

Locating Russian's war within a global context, The Zelensky Method is unsparing in its critique of those nations, who have refused to condemn Russia's invasion and are doing everything they can to prevent economic sanctions from being imposed on the Kremlin.

China & Europe: The Turning Point
by David Baverez

In creating five fictitious conversations between Xi Jinping and five European experts, David Baverez, who lives and works in Hong Kong, offers up a totally new vision of the relationship between China and Europe.

Masonic Myths and Legends
by Pierre Mollier

Freemasonry is one of the few organizations whose teaching method is still based on symbols. It presents these symbols by inserting them into legends that are told to its members in initiation ceremonies. But its history itself has also given rise to a whole mythology.

Resistance: Reflections on Survival, Hope and Love
Poetry by William Morris, Photography by Jackie Malden

Resistance is a book of poems with photographs or a book of photographs with poems depending on your perspective. The book is comprised of three sections titled respectively: On Survival, On Hope, and On Love.

Bunker Diplomacy: An Arab-American in the U.S. Foreign Service
by Nabeel Khoury

After twenty-five years in the Foreign Service, Dr. Nabeel A. Khoury retired from the U.S. Department of State in 2013 with the rank of Minister Counselor. In his last overseas posting, Khoury served as deputy chief of mission at the U.S. embassy in Yemen (2004-2007).

Managing Challenges for the Flint Water Crisis
Edited by Toyna E. Thornton, Andrew D. Williams, Katherine M. Simon, Jennifer F. Sklarew

This edited volume examines several public management and intergovernmental failures, with particular attention on social, political, and financial impacts. Understanding disaster meaning, even causality, is essential to the problem-solving process.

Donald J. Trump, The 45th U.S. Presidency and Beyond International Perspectives
Editors: John Dixon and Max J. Skidmore

The reality is that throughout Trump's presidency, there was a clearly perceptible decline of his—and America's—global standing, which accelerated as an upshot of his mishandling of both the Corvid-19 pandemic and his 2020 presidential election loss.

Brought to Light: The Mysterious George Washington Masonic Cave
by Jason Williams, MD

The George Washington Masonic Cave near Charles Town, West Virginia, contains a signature carving of George Washington dated 1748. Although this inscription appears authentic, it has yet to be verified by historical accounts or scientific inquiry.

Abortion and Informed Common Sense
by Max J. Skidmore

The controversy over a woman's "right to choose," as opposed to the numerous "rights" that abortion opponents decide should be assumed to exist for "unborn children," has always struck me as incomplete. Two missing elements of the argument seems obvious, yet they remain almost completely overlooked.

The Athenian Year Primer: Attic Time-Reckoning and the Julian Calendar
by Christopher Planeaux

The ability to translate ancient Athenian calendar references into precise Julian-Gregorian dates will not only assist Ancient Historians and Classicists to date numerous historical events with much greater accuracy but also aid epigraphists in the restorations of numerous Attic inscriptions.

The Politics of Fiscal Responsibility: A Comparative Perspective
by Tonya E. Thornton and F. Stevens Redburn

Fiscal policy challenges following the Great Recession forced members of the Organisation for Economic Co-operation and Development (OECD) to implement a set of economic policies to manage public debt.

Growing Inequality: Bridging Complex Systems, Population Health, and Health Disparities
Editors: George A. Kaplan, Ana V. Diez Roux, Carl P. Simon, and Sandro Galea

Why is America's health is poorer than the health of other wealthy countries and why health inequities persist despite our efforts? In this book, researchers report on groundbreaking insights to simulate how these determinants come together to produce levels of population health and disparities and test new solutions.

Issues in Maritime Cyber Security
Edited by Dr. Joe DiRenzo III, Dr. Nicole K. Drumhiller, and Dr. Fred S. Roberts

The complexity of making MTS safe from cyber attack is daunting and the need for all stakeholders in both government (at all levels) and private industry to be involved in cyber security is more significant than ever as the use of the MTS continues to grow.

A Radical In The East
by S. Brent Morris, PhD

The papers presented here represent over twenty-five years of publications by S. Brent Morris. They explore his many questions about Freemasonry, usually dealing with origins of the Craft. A complex organization with a lengthy pedigree like Freemasonry has many basic foundational questions waiting to be answered, and that's what this book does: answers questions.

Contests of Initiative: Countering China's Gray Zone Strategy in the East and South China Seas
by Dr. Raymond Kuo

China is engaged in a widespread assertion of sovereignty in the South and East China Seas. It employs a "gray zone" strategy: using coercive but sub-conventional military power to drive off challengers and prevent escalation, while simultaneously seizing territory and asserting maritime control.

Frontline Diplomacy: A Memoir of a Foreign Service Officer in the Middle East
by William A. Rugh

In short vignettes, this book describes how American diplomats working in the Middle East dealt with a variety of challenges over the last decades of the 20th century. Each of the vignettes concludes with an insight about diplomatic practice derived from the experience.

Anti-Poverty Measures in America: Scientism and Other Obstacles
Editors, Max J. Skidmore and Biko Koenig

Anti-Poverty Measures in America brings together a remarkable collection of essays dealing with the inhibiting effects of scientism, an over-dependence on scientific methodology that is prevalent in the social sciences, and other obstacles to anti-poverty legislation.

Geopolitics of Outer Space: Global Security and Development
by Ilayda Aydin

A desire for increased security and rapid development is driving nation-states to engage in an intensifying competition for the unique assets of space. This book analyses the Chinese-American space discourse from the lenses of international relations theory, history and political psychology to explore these questions.

westphaliapress.org

Made in USA - North Chelmsford, MA
1328770_9781637239179